Daughter of the Town

Miriam C. Crouch

Black Rose Writing | Texas

First printing

This is a work of fiction. Names, characters, businesses, places, events, and incidents are either the products of the author's imagination or used in a fictitious manner. Any resemblance to actual persons, living or dead, or actual events is purely coincidental.

ISBN: 978-1-68433-219-9
PUBLISHED BY BLACK ROSE WRITING
www.blackrosewriting.com

Printed in the United States of America
Suggested Retail Price (SRP) $17.95

Daughter of the Town is printed in Plantagenet Cherokee

Daughter of the Town

Chapter 1. Deep in the Heart

It's the familiar whistle of the 7:25 right on time tonight. I'm usually here in my office on the edge of downtown every night, so I am quite aware of the train schedule although being on time is rare. Don't try to set your watch by that train. As I gaze at the dusky twilight darkening over the towering skyscrapers, I give in to my yearning for reassurance that everything will work out. After all, I remind myself, remember how far you have come. Sometimes my sanity begs for relief: to live in this world, I need to escape to another world.

That darn train. I have a bad case of nostalgia creeping over me and now that thing. Right now, it seems almost anything would take me back. Think of it. That historic iron horse brought progress and development to our enormous unconnected country much of it wilderness. It transports, connects, intersects and divides. When we were kids, we couldn't get enough. We played on the tracks, put our ears to the ground to listen for the roaring sound of its arrival, memorized the ETAs, waited and watched for a wave from the engineer who gave us that thrill: his long-anticipated broad grin and toot of his whistle. We counted the cars and imagined what was inside and planted ourselves alongside the tracks to watch until the caboose was out of sight. We saw ourselves hopping on and off like kangaroos seeing the world riding the rails from one breath-taking adventure to the next. The rails enticed us almost as much as the train. It was a temptation that none of us could resist no matter how often our parents insisted we stay away. The seduction of that massive marvel of transportation was too strong. It transported us to a faraway place only limited by our imaginations.

The tracks also served as a marker. It separated the preferred side of town where I lived from the other, poorer side. That's not to say that there weren't some nice houses and some nice people on the other side, it was just an accepted principle of social strata and another major cultural hurdle. On the other side, most of the houses were rundown and filled with transients. These people were not claimed as residents of our town. They rented for the month and then moved on unnoticed and unimportant for the most part. Some were vagrants who sought shelter for a night or two. My lifetime friend Libby came from the other side of the tracks and spent most of her life trying to overcome the stigma.

In my fifteen years as a family law attorney, while I'm not hardened to clients' troubles, I have become somewhat well-seasoned. The case I have just closed has taken its toll. I've represented hundreds of troubled families through the entanglements of divorce, child custody, child support and adoption proceedings but this one was particularly difficult because it hit too close to home. A single mother dying of breast cancer with four children ages two to nine came to us for help to keep her children out of foster care after her death. Michael and I contacted everyone we knew to try to keep the children together, but we could not make it happen. The family had to be split up and the children placed in three separate homes throughout the country. The resemblance to the family turmoil of my best friend Libby has brought back all the old heartache of my ten-year-old Claire self.

The days of my youth happened so fast that they seem like yesterday. Yet they began so long ago that I think of my early days as antediluvian. I grew up in a small Texas town in the 1950s and 60s and early on had a keen sense of my surroundings and the people in it. Therefore, large chunks of who I am I can readily trace back to people or events that took hold of my character forcibly and relentlessly. My closest friend and I shared an inexplicable lifetime bond that began almost immediately like two young ivy sprouts intertwining. She is a part of my being, and therefore she shares a significant part of my story. I believe we are as close to being one person as two people can be yet we are opposites. In my dream of dreams, I'd soar with no boundaries with one caveat—my feet on the ground. I know. It's not going to happen. Libby has her eye on the prize; she will take the risk. So there you have it. In spite of or perhaps *because* of our differences, we are inseparable.

I was adopted as an infant by a respected small town lawyer and his wife. I was accustomed to being doted on and having my own way and never knew anything other than a secure, stable and sheltered life. As I began my school years, so began the process of losing my childhood innocence much like a baby bird being jolted out of its warm nest. I smile when I think of that young girl so full of herself and her ideals. As with most of us, my values, goals and dreams seemed to come effortlessly; it was the follow through that proved difficult. I made agonizing decisions and others almost carelessly. Many of my reactions and decisions to events and people melted into my being so naturally along with my conscious, deliberate ones that I was oblivious as to how or why I became the person I was.

My best friend Libby came into my life at age ten. I remember those days with both painful memories and moments of hopeful exuberance. In contrast to my life of ease, she had struggled to survive and had coped with the ravages of abuse and rejection, broken family ties as well as the physical challenges of hunger and poverty. She longed for acceptance in a world where she was ostracized, isolated and constantly looked down upon and rejected as unworthy. A local ranch family adopted her when her mother could no longer support her and her siblings. We shared those days as she dealt with continuing conflict and the emotional trauma of guilt, aloneness, and abandonment when she was forced to give up her family whom she adored. Her new life of material comfort and security came with a price; she had to give up her family *and* she had no emotional connection to her new family. By the age of ten, she was a child of a broken home twice. My heart ached for her. I did what I could—be the best friend possible and always be there for her—as I watched my friend search for revival and renewal and her place in the world. It was a question that continued to haunt me. Can there be rebirth of a child's spirit so far gone at such a young age? During her journey, our dedication to each other and our trust and loyalty served us well. Our friendship based on love, respect, and belief in each other sustained us.

We learned from each other as our friendship flourished through the conflicts and challenges we faced. I found myself floundering in dark waters thrust from my predictable world of perfection—shocked and wounded. My family unit ceased to exist. I experienced some of what Libby had gone through. Helplessness did not suit me. When I looked at Libby, I saw a tough cookie. I decided being someone to be reckoned with was definitely not all bad. I wanted to be like her.

Today Libby is dedicated to education and helping children. She is also worldly, street-smart and intuitive, kind and caring. But it has taken her a lifetime to make the trip across those tracks to overcome the second-class label she chose to accept for many years. She set her sights high and is living proof that it is possible to re-image to effect positive personal change.

It's part of our nature to be driven to strive for better no matter our origins. I'm not saying our lives are perfect or even perfectly figured out. What is reflected is the process of change and growth. We are forced into life's arena no matter from which side of the tracks we come. We are faced with crossroads, obstacles and decisions whether we develop our coping skills early or on an urgent, as-needed basis.

My first major personal struggle forced me to deal with debilitating disease and death that struck my family. The nightmare continued as deceit and betrayal arose from within my family. I watched helplessly as my world of traditional values was turned upside down. I was unprepared for personal tragedy and had to learn to cope with events out of my control. Throughout hard times particularly, I learned to confront my own weaknesses and those of my parents and to take the next step in the process—forgiveness. I began to understand the power within. I had grossly underestimated my belief in the Higher Power. I began to understand the strength that a capacity to love and be loved gives us. Some of us who pride ourselves on operating solo and envision being in complete control seem destined to learn this lesson in the midst of trouble when we seek the answers and peace no one can give us. I learned firsthand that there is no one to bail me out. I was abandoned by my own human frailty that could not prevail against these defining moments.

My parents showed me it is possible to be driven to succeed and to live a meaningful life through their contributions and involvement in the community that resulted in positive, substantive change. Whether social or personal change, transformations rarely if ever just happen. Change is made by taking a stand even if difficult and/or unpopular and takes planning, sacrifice, hard work and hard decisions. My turning point came bundled up in a package of selfishness that is best described by the simple phrase: I want what I want when I want it *regardless.* This familiar, often chronic condition threatened conflict and destruction that could have marked me as *beyond redemption.*

The world's tumultuous events of the 60s had a crushing impact on my generation. We were continuously bombarded. Riots and widespread destruction were commonplace because of our inhumanity to each other and prolonged segregation. We suffered through years of a war that devastated families, divided our Nation and cost us thousands of lives plus devastating injuries, illness and disease suffered by our veterans from the effects of exposure to Agent Orange. We never knew who would be next to be struck down by an assassin's bullet. No leader or crusader was immune no matter the stature or how beloved. Our youthful optimism was overshadowed by years of turmoil, social unrest, hopelessness and chaos that threatened our country. Even more troubling is the drug culture of the 60s which infested our society and took roots—now our Nation's most evil self-invasive foe. Every generation has its darkness to face, and we were no exception.

All these lasting effects of family, friendship, community and world dynamics as building blocks of our character shape us as human beings. In retrospect, I see a story of hope and inspiration and the power of love as lives converge—no matter the time, the place or the generation. My life took on a new awakening as I experienced ranch life with Libby. In the small town where I grew up, the ranches were the heart and soul of our town. I learned to revere and connect to the land so plentiful around me and to appreciate the lives that touched and inspired me. Slowly and painfully, I learned to believe in myself. My life has been filled with His blessings and people who care. Even in hard times, I have been sustained.

I treasure those memories of growing up in Texas during a period now extinct. It's a journey from across both sides of the tracks that just happened to take place in a little country town—deep in my heart and deep in the heart of Texas.

Chapter 2. Pop. 1274

It's a place with its own special spirit. What some people abhor as suffocating, others find fulfilling and sustaining—the small town. It was a spot in the road like hundreds of other Texas towns; just a boring, nondescript place in the highway in the way of your way to get to someplace important. We were an aggravation rather than an enticement to stop. The stranger behind the wheel posed the biggest hazard for a small child like me as he sped through town. The traffic light (often ignored) still forced a motorist to make a split second decision to stop or risk being ticketed by our local sheriff. It was not a hard decision for most drivers who filled our coffer with easy revenue from running reds and speeding. Our town (as the county seat) was built around a square with magnificent oak trees and a beautiful old turn-of-the-century stone courthouse. Strictly judging by appearance, an outsider would refer to our town as typical with our twang, slang, dialect and drawl, the rhythm of our town was hopelessly Texan.

Once you got to know us, there definitely was substance to us and our town. Peeling back the layers to reveal the unique qualities of my town or any town takes effort. Most drive-by visitors had neither the time nor the inclination. In contrast, as a child who was fascinated by what lie beyond, I could not wait to explore this world. Ultimately I was the culmination of that experience. I became a part of the heartbeat of a community—the one thousand, two hundred and seventy-four souls who called this *home*. As I reflect on childhood days that I remember with great affection, I can understand why young people today would call it the dark ages compared to today's world which is indistinguishable from my childhood world and arguably in many respects, not in a positive way. It was truly retro town, and I loved it. We could not wish for a better place to live. Granted, most of us had not ventured far beyond its city limits. We accepted and were unfazed that we were terminally unsophisticated and far short of cosmopolitan and were seen as hicks by outsiders (especially from the city). As country dwellers, we claimed the treasure that did not diminish but increased in value with time. The source of our arrogance? The bounty lie wide open for all to see in the miles and miles of rolling grassland home to thousands of Hereford and Angus cattle, goats, and sheep. Whether a few acres or thousands, the pride of ownership runs deep. We revere the land. A limited supply of a precious commodity was embodied in our simple, familiar phrase: there's no infinite amount of land, you can't make anymore. The love of land translates to value not measured merely in dollars and cents. Although as an investment, it's rare to find its equal. Land values continually increase at unbelievable rates—that is a given. There is a catch. Hard times come to most of us and holding onto the land for dear life while passionate may not be economically feasible. Throughout history, our philosophy did not waver that land was the one wise and worthwhile lifetime investment. Accumulate as much of it as your bank account and your banker would allow.

For those of us who lived in town, we were surrounded by our own temptations and knew every nook and cranny that lured us to have fun. The swimming pool had been closed for a couple of years due to the polio outbreak but now was open again. It was the coolest place in the summer if you could withstand a pool full of screaming six-to twelve-year-olds. There was a pond and small fountain in the park hidden under the massive shade trees. At the beginning of summer, it was a haven to splash and play for the younger kids. By July, the pond dried to cakey black mud, perfect for mud fights. The fountain was put there (at least in our minds) for us to cool off. The closest lake for water skiing was thirty miles away and was an occasional treat.

Kids were on the baseball field and on their bikes. This was a great season to be a kid and a great place to explore. No traffic, no worries, seemingly endless adventure. There was one rule. Take off on your bike in the morning—fine—but you must be back before supper. Our summers were filled with picnics and barbeques, fishing in the creek, lazy days with no schedule except for mandatory Vacation Bible School, and numerous slumber parties. The relentless Texas heat did not faze us. The constant complaining of the old folks about the heat and lack of rain fell on deaf ears making us stubbornly determined to enjoy every minute. I wondered if I ever wanted to grow up. It seemed to me that adults rarely were genuinely happy about anything and mostly dissatisfied about everything. That fact intensified our efforts to immerse ourselves in a world of freedom, fun, and total self-indulgence for at least three months a year.

Kids sat at the marble counter in the drugstore drinking all kinds of sweet, thick, tasty concoctions in tall, frosty mugs. With our legs swinging and stools twirling at top speed, we raced to go faster until someone fell off or the guy wearing the funny white hat behind the counter lost all patience. He might be known as a soda jerk, but only a fool who never wanted another ice cream would call him that to his face. The wood floors, after decades of abuse and wear, were so old and creaky they seemed to buckle under the weight of the smallest child. I stared at the ceilings captivated by the maze of shiny tin-stamped squares of interlocking patterns. Ceiling fans whirled nonstop at incredible speed keeping the store cool and comfortable. No air conditioning, no problem. The smooth coolness of the swirls of green marble on my hot arms filled me with an uncontrollable urge to jump on the counter belly side down. I wisely resisted the urge and was content with my cold and buttery, sweet treat…heavenly velvet ice cream in a choice of flavors.

My parents' offices faced the courthouse. They shared a small two-story building with the insurance agency run by Jim Haggerty and his wife Millie and a wide-eyed blonde receptionist named Lorene. My dad, being *the* lawyer in town, had one of the prime locations on the square. Next door was the bank with its tiny octagonal white and black tile floors and teller windows with brass bars and marble counters. On the other side was our 85-year-old dentist Dr. Shackleford who specialized in keeping you in suspense with tools older than he was and the attention span of a gnat. As he steadfastly gazed out the window to the courthouse, while you were having a tooth filled or even worse, he seemed to forget that you were held hostage in his century-old dental chair that looked like a leftover from the Spanish Inquisition.

Along the west side flanked the hardware store proudly displaying as much of its inventory as possible on the sidewalk. Bicycles, air conditioners, lawn mowers and garden tools were strewn everywhere. The two grocery stores faced off opposite sides of the square as if doing battle which they often did. Their store windows were covered with paper advertising price cuts and specials to the delight of their customers. The downtown café where Dad and his cronies had coffee every morning and afternoon like clockwork was on the south side. On the end was the post office, with its tiny glass and combination lock boxes where most of us got our mail and served as a daily meet and greet your neighbors.

The town newspaper called the Gazette run by Mr. Kipperson was a favorite spot for me. I loved to watch the weekly paper fly through the printing press as I strained to see through the top half of a Dutch door kept open so that the stinky ink escaped to permeate the air. The farm-to-market road heading north had a large assortment of businesses with one of my favorites, the large dry goods store called the Mercantile, the five and dime, two service stations and our one movie theater. The crossroads whether to continue on the state highway or turn on the farm-to-market road was regulated by the one traffic light. Our lake was small but picture book hidden away in groves of live oaks. Out the state highway five miles from town on a hill (a high point for this part of Texas), our state park overlooking the town nestled the small placid lake. No motorboats were allowed, only fishing boats, a somewhat unusual type of lake, calm and serene. Teen dances and picnics were popular at the pavilion complete with jukebox. About the only thing missing from our small lake was Frankie and Annette. The music was great, the scenery perfection and the energy was full throttle, but the parties were predictable and far short of expectation. The girls danced with each other, and the boys sat bored to distraction for an obligatory hour or so and then they disappeared to find some action with girls in the upper class.

Across from the school, town and school gatherings were held in the small recreation center. The swimming pool was nearby, and there were two clay tennis courts full of bumps, cracks and uneven settling adding extra hazards to a match divided by a saggy net full of holes. The track and field area adjacent to the high school and the gymnasium was a complete but aging complex that we had no idea of how second-rate until we went away to college.

Once we were licensed to drive, we congregated at the drive-in hamburger stand outside town about two miles. The round trip to cruise through the four sides of town and to the burger place took fifteen minutes. The burning of gasoline was a rite of passage. At 35 cents a gallon, even though our cars were gas guzzlers, it was a fairly reasonable value for the dollar. The girls were cruising to find the cute (and older) guys. The guys were itching for a drag race *and* girls. I did not have a car in high school but Sherilyn, in exchange for doing her older sister's domestic chores, got to borrow her 1955 Bel Air. Otherwise, I would have missed most of Cruising 101. Every aspect of our young lives revolved around cars so that would have been definitive teen cruelty.

My mom and dad worked long hours most days of the week. During my younger years, I spent my after-school hours in their office staying out of their way by playing in the storage room among the files, papers and supplies. It was dark and musty with all the smells of out of sight, out of mind that was akin to grandma's attic. I read my books and spent hours playing make-believe with my dolls. I developed early my favorite pastime of eavesdropping on my parents' phone conversations. "Yes, Mr. Brown, your *Will* will be ready for you to sign this Friday. You can read and make any changes then." I strained to hear the legal words to build my vocabulary to impress my peers and make me feel superior. Snooping was taboo, so naturally I was hooked. I had been warned repeatedly about confidentiality. Mother was quick to remind me, "Our clients depend on us to keep their business private. We don't talk outside this office about what goes on here at work." She spent a lot of her time on the telephone so that Dad could "draft" documents, go to court, take witness statements and depositions and do the important legal work. Mother typed my dad's dictation, scheduled all his court and client appointments and kept his calendar of appearances and paperwork deadlines. They worked like gee and haw. Mother occasionally allowed me to help with simple tasks such as mailing and stamping letters and assembling documents or collate as she called it and going to the post office or making bank deposits. I memorized the legal terms I heard my dad use, saying them over and over so that I could impress my friends especially Travis Wayne. Smart aleck, show him.

I was named for my paternal grandmother Nadia Cathleen Chastain whom I do not remember and my mother Nella Claire. My grandmother was a widow at the age of forty-five and continued to run the dry goods store after my grandfather passed away. My dad helped her in the store and then went on to study law and came back to open his law office and take care of his mother. She died when I was three years old. He and Mother were high school sweethearts and married shortly after he opened his law practice. At the beginning, he did mostly wills and simple real estate documents. As the years passed, his probate practice involved complex trusts and, with the prospering land business, his real estate practice flourished. Lawsuits were rare and generally involved land boundaries or contracts with the occasional Hatfield and McCoy dispute involving neighbors who couldn't get along. He, as a natural mediator, was well-known for his ability to get people to compromise. Costly lawsuits resulted in big outlays of cash and hard feelings and resentment eventually were settled amicably although these differences were rarely resolved quickly and easily. Getting people to come together much less agree to anything was time-consuming, frustrating, and far from profitable. He and Mother worked as a team to build their business and reputation, but they both wanted a family. Mother had been told early on that the odds were against her being able to have children.

After years of trying, she began to accept the reality. After a series of tests, the city doctor confirmed the country doctor's opinion. They decided to adopt. When I was about five, they explained to me that I was adopted. I was one week old when they brought me home. A young mother from a neighboring town had given me up for adoption within a few hours of my birth. Nadia Claire Chastain became the center of the universe for John and Nella Chastain. They were unequivocally my parents. I never questioned or wished otherwise, and I was not the least bit curious about my birth mother. I was a Chastain. Nella Claire was my beloved mother—beginning and end of story. I would not have been any more their daughter if I had been born to them. I dared anyone to suggest otherwise.

Chapter 3. Beyond the City Limits

Town was my playground. I seldom had a babysitter and was admittedly spoiled but not with material things. I was covetous of my precious time. I did not have grandparents, and I did not willingly tolerate someone taking care of me or dictating how I spent my days. I liked being on my own to roam. I went to the drugstore and had ice cream and to the movies, and to the five and dime because the old lady in there liked children and welcomed the company. I liked to hear her talk about the olden days when she was a girl like me. Mother laughed that she recognized most of the same merchandise as being in that store when she was a kid.

I longed to go into the Mercantile because it was a magical store and because I was banned. The man who owned it was a grump and made it clear: off-limits to children. It seemed he intentionally lured me to come in tempting me with every exquisite, sparkling or shiny object imaginable. I had to be content to stare in the enormous plate glass showcase meticulously decorated and sparkling clean. Chic mannequins gazed afar with their perfect and sculptured blank faces. Aloof and untouchable, they towered above me adorned from head to toe with stylish clothing and accessories which he spent hours dressing and re-dressing down to the smallest detail. Gentlemen's outfits were finished with flourish. A surprise accessory you would never see a man wear around here—a wool scarf looped and then artfully cascaded across the shoulder, lambskin leather gloves or a fashionable umbrella or walking cane—was style for a New York dandy. The mannequins flaunted their fashions adorned with coiffed wigs and outlandish costume jewelry down to their coordinated high heel pumps and matching handbags. At Christmas, it was a stampede for the grand viewing of our own splashy copycat New York display. Every inch of the large Mercantile windows glistened with lights, snow and greenery showcasing ice skaters, carolers and other Christmas scenes highlighted by a mechanical Santa and Mrs. Claus. His intent to outshine every other store and be the talk of the town was his other tradition along with his strict policy of no children.

We ate many of our meals at the downtown café and occasionally at the hamburger joint. If it had been left to me, I would have existed on hamburgers, chili dogs and chocolate malts from the Dairy Mart. One of Mother's greatest annoyances was me ordering a hamburger when we went to the restaurant to have a "nice dinner."

I felt important because everyone knew who I was and who my parents were, and it was imperative that I know everyone and call them by name. My parents did not tolerate disrespect whether towards people, animals or property, and they demanded kindness. I was expected to mind my Ps and Qs. In a town this size, any misbehavior got back to my parents at supersonic speed. "We live with these people, we work for and with these people and we need each other," my mother reminded me. "I know, Mother. I want them to like me, too." I had an ulterior motive. My future was here. I was so happy I never wanted to live anywhere else.

Many of the high school graduates and the college-bound seniors liked to call it a one-horse town or Hicksville or some other disparaging name. They intended to find their fame and fortune anywhere but here. In my child's mind, I had formulated my plans. I planned to go to the state college, get my law degree and come back to practice law with my dad. I thought that I had formulated the perfect life. Unlike some of my peers, I wanted to get an education and was curious about life outside this little berg. I did not intend to be one of those people who peaks at sixteen, marries a local yokel, and has a kid hanging from every extremity. Not to mention being someone who thinks of a trip as spending the day in a neighboring town. I had higher hopes for myself. My parents drilled into me the importance of education, being prepared, and taking advantage of opportunity. I planned to do just that and then come back to my town transformed into *somebody. Just like my dad.*

Chapter 4. *Virginia*

The faces and places are crystal clear, and their impact is staggering. My early memories are vivid of precisely what I did and where I went; the people whose paths I crossed; and the emotionally-charged events of my youth. Of course, there were many other experiences that helped to carve me out as the person I would become, but particular people from my youth left their indelible imprint on me—an innocent and impressionable young Claire stepping into the world beyond. It seemed strange at first, but I eventually acknowledged that I took up a smaller and increasingly insignificant place on the planet. I might have been the center of the Chastain universe and the daughter of the town's leading citizen, but that would be the last moments any world would revolve around me. I relished my somewhat fabricated superior position in my small world, but I began to realize its limitations and resigned myself to its constraints and acknowledged that I must move on.

As I entered first grade, if challenged to do so, I could close my eyes and pretty much recite the names of the people in my class and maybe even where they chose to sit, sight unseen. My pre-school friends Sherilyn and Laurie would be in my class. Small town, small classes, mostly synonymous with predictable. Those thirty students might increase to forty through the school years but, whoever was with you in first grade, peek under the graduation caps twelve years later and they were still there. The prospect of starting "big" school was still exciting in spite of knowing my classmates beforehand. First grade was memorable for many reasons. The magnitude of it all was encompassed in a small six-year-old stranger who entered our classroom and my life. She was one of the dearest friends I ever had and one who had a profound and lasting effect on me. After our friendship, I was a changed young girl. It was my first conscious marker of growing up. I was hurled without warning from my safe place into the world of the unknown and a lifetime of questioning—the whys without answers. The first day of first grade, Sherilyn, Laurie and I were sitting on the front row when Ginny came in. I couldn't keep from staring. I was attracted to her instantly. She was delicate and small—doll-like—with short, curly blond hair and clear dark blue eyes. Shy and unsure, she walked in with her eyes glued downward. I saw her hands shaking. She is scared, I thought, and I wondered why. Then I thought of how I would feel coming into a room of strangers with all those *eyes*.

Mrs. Robbins put her arm gently around Ginny as she presented her to our class, "Let's all welcome Virginia to our school. She and her family just moved here from Louisiana."

One little boy yelled out, "Bet she's one of them Cajuns my dad talks about."

Mrs. Robbins looked at him disapprovingly and continued, "There will be no yelling out in my classroom. Virginia, there is a seat for you next to Claire."

I smiled at her and motioned to the desk next to me. I decided she was going to be my new friend. We ate lunch together and spent every recess playing. The most remarkable thing about her was that she (like me) loved to read. That was the foundation of our friendship that not only withstood the stress of her illness but thrived. We spent almost every Sunday together. She went to church with us and then we had lunch and spent the day playing and reading books. We enjoyed our Sundays, our quiet time, for almost three years. Then the unthinkable happened. In the summer after the third grade, Ginny got sick.

I continued to look forward to being with her. I visited my friend at least once a week usually on Wednesday after school and some Sundays. She did not go to school or church or to ballgames, the movies or to visit friends. Ginny lived in an iron lung. She had been on the verge of death at the age of eight stricken by the most dreaded contagious viral infection of the century, poliomyelitis. Her lungs were permanently paralyzed, and now she lay ravaged by its cruelty with no hope of ever breathing on her own. Her parents took her out of the machine for a few hours each day, but it was an exhausting and laborious procedure, hardly worth the effort. She had been confined for two years and tolerated her new surroundings as permanent. She accepted the giant iron cocoon as secure and somewhat comforting after her daily struggle to stay on the outside for a few hours. She found the outside increasingly terrifying as she labored to breathe. I was in awe that I took such a simple process for granted with never a thought. But I learned by watching Ginny that there is nothing simple about breathing. Breathing ultimately is a complicated function requiring all the necessary elements in perfect rhythm. It seems simple if it functions naturally, uninterrupted and uncomplicated, and impeccably syncopated. This was my first experience seeing the dysfunction of the human body, and my acknowledgment of the miracle we are.

I brought what I could of the outside world such as books and tales of schoolmates and what had happened in school. She tolerated my foolish distractions, but she was most profoundly interested in the books I had brought. Her eyes would star twinkle and dance as I started to read aloud. Her face beamed with eagerness and new life. We read. We re-read and re-hashed. We were transfixed that we would never run out of adventure. The books of our youth were there for our taking—*Alice's Adventures in Wonderland, Jane Eyre, A Tree Grows in Brooklyn, Her Father's Daughter,* and *Forever Amber.* Our most exciting and ambitious project lie ahead. We were determined that *Gone with the Wind* would be next on our list and were not intimidated by either the bulk or content of the text.

Her parents owned a small grocery store and gas station that was open twelve hours a day. Other than one part-time helper, her mom and dad worked day and night and also took care of Virginia. The sugary sweetness penetrated the air as I opened the screen door to the store. As part of our ritual, I picked one jelly doughnut for us to share. Sugar was on the limited list, but this was an exception. Having to choose from the variety of raspberry, lemon, pineapple, and cherry flavors was a task I relished. We hurriedly stuffed down our sweet so that we could dive into our adventure.

We couldn't wait to tell each other about what we read, talking at the same time and then giggling that we didn't know what each other said. There wasn't much that we missed in a book. Sometimes I barely managed a few words: "I couldn't believe" or "that was not what I expected" to describe my reaction to our reading. What I was interested in was what she thought. There was a clear and understandable reason for this. Ginny would take the lead in our discussion, and I was fascinated as she unfolded the story and any underlying meanings easily. Ginny astounded and enlightened me with her thoughts that I had completely overlooked. She and I agreed that we wanted to be writers and, as she often reminded me, "I think the more books you read, the better writer you will be."

Ginny hardly ever talked about her misfortune. She admitted that the effects from polio would not improve and that she must endure them. Yet she was filled with hope. She confided that, as unrealistic as it seemed, she clung to that hope and often dreamed that she would awaken and be well. The hope she embraced the most was that a cure would be found so that others would be saved. I continually wondered at her strength, and I was amazed at the adjustment and acceptance required of my nine-year-old friend. As difficult as her life became, she continued to embrace each day. As I reflect on those days, her strength of will and refusal to give in to hopelessness still inspire and astound me. I never saw her cry in self-pity. I never saw a dark cloud of moodiness surround her.

Much to our dismay, Margaret Mitchell had to wait. We did not finish our beloved southern epic. We were knee deep in Scarlett and Rhett at the benefit dance for the Confederacy in Atlanta when Rhett won his bid for a dance with Scarlett. We would not finish the story.

I recognized the monumental impact of her illness and of our relationship. Without warning, she became critically ill and was hospitalized for three long, agonizing weeks. I forced myself to go to the hospital. I was miserable when I went to see her, and I was miserable when I did not go. She lapsed into a coma and would never awaken. Day after day she lay there, and day after day I prayed and longed for her to improve. Her parents were on the verge of collapse. Then it hit me. Think about her parents, not yourself. Do you think they want to see their daughter suffer? I saw my part in this seemingly endless ordeal drastically change. Certainly, it was questionable whether Ginny was aware that I was with her. But there was another consideration. Her parents needed me now. I fought my selfish thoughts of how much I was hurting and how much she and her family were suffering and there should be an end to her suffering now. It was not in my power.

My parents and I provided the comfort and support we could. At the ripe old age of nine, I experienced being in the throes of a desperate, hopeless situation in which I was powerless. I had no control and no solution. We could not change those circumstances, but we could do our best for Ginny and her parents. I tried to cope with the loss but what seemed even more difficult were the tragic circumstances. I grappled with the despair and questioning of seeing my friend and her family suffer during her struggle with the effects of polio, her long illness and ultimately her death. I was not the same little girl. I learned it was an inevitable part of living—the purity and innocence of childhood destined to be stripped away by reality.

Ginny's dream did come true. In 1955, the polio vaccine made possible by researcher Dr. Jonas Salk was made available which was a miracle for us all especially the children of the 50s. A monster of our childhood days had been defeated. I have carried the image of Ginny and her inspiration with me my entire life. Likewise, the unresolved conflict of a suffering child remains.

Ginny realized she would not have the opportunity to grow old. Yet she imagined what it might be like to live a long, full life. We decided the wisdom gained from costly mistakes may come with longevity but mostly from experiences or *character builders* which determine the depth of a person's wisdom and understanding, not merely age. Ginny already was a wise old soul far beyond her years.

I have often thought about Ginny that she did not have the luxury of time. She was forced to learn *what she was made of* early and without warning. Many of us may live a lifetime before we know. I smile when I think of her and am forever thankful for her inspired life touching mine. She loved this passage which never failed to make us laugh. Ginny recited it easily, and I can still hear her small, clear voice:

> "You are old, father William," the young man said,
> "And your hair has become very white;
> And yet you incessantly stand on your head—
> Do you think, at your age, it is right?"
>
> "In my youth," father William replied to his son,
> "I feared it might injure my brain;
> But now that I'm perfectly sure I have none,
> Why, I do it again and again."
> *Lewis Carroll, Alice's Adventures in Wonderland*

Chapter 5. Annalee Masters

While I was running amuck in the four corners, Mother spent most of her days working at their law office. I tried to stay out of major trouble and out of her hair. She had a full day with work and home and seeing about me. She had suffered from headaches for as long as I could remember; I wondered if I was the cause. She called them migraines. As she got older, the frequency and intensity of her headaches increased which required her to go to bed. The doctor encouraged her to take time for herself, so when she did have the luxury to be at home, she relaxed by playing her piano. She had played all her life and could have been a concert pianist, anyone who knew her and her playing would tell you. When she played the piano, everything stood still. She could play any type of music. I sat on the stool beside her so that I could watch her beautiful, long fingers fly across the keys. She could hear a song and, in a few minutes with the keyboard, she played the song without any sheet music. Dad laughed and said he played the violin as a fiddle and sometimes after supper he and mother played duets. It was my favorite time. They played mostly country tunes because that's what my dad could play, but they would try almost any kind of music. Our little house seemed to bounce with the beat of pure joy.

Dad teased me saying, "All we need are some flat-footers and cloggers."

He saw my puzzled look.

"Those are dancers, Claire. My grandparents from Virginia used to tear up the floor. They were quite a sight."

I watched and listened to their voices resonate and to their free and spontaneous laughter with their eyes bright with love and flirtation. They lit up the room whether they were singing duets or teasing each other with their banter of conversation during mealtime. I believed Nella and John Chastain were truly a match made in heaven. They didn't always agree, and their personalities were polar opposites, but they complemented each other to perfection. I loved hearing Mother play their song, *Stardust.* It was as if Hoagy Carmichael had taken over the keys with her soft, throaty voice in accompaniment. There was no doubt. My parents were in love.

It was Mother's dream that I would be a pianist, and Annalee Masters was the key to seeing that dream fulfilled. Mother began early preparing me for my twice weekly piano lessons. I think I remember as early as age four sitting with her at the piano as she placed my small fingers on the keys hoping for some sign of musical genius or even a smidgen of wonder or excitement.

Miss Masters was a really old, old maid. When I began piano lessons at age six, she was old and wrinkled with a distinctive unpleasant smell about her. I could hardly make myself sit next to her as she repeatedly hit my fingers with her pointer stick whenever I hit a sour note. When I complained to my mother about the smell, she stiffened and cleared her throat. Then she looked directly in my eyes and said with a straight face, "Miss Masters is an extremely clean person."

The other kids and I soon figured it out without any grown-up assistance. Miss Masters was a human mothball. My friend Laurie, who was also roped into taking piano against her will, was the whiz kid who eventually zeroed in on the smell. "That's the same smell my sweaters have when Mom takes them out when it gets cold every year. Miss Masters is preserved—in mothballs!"

We all rolled in laughter. But it didn't solve our problem. We still had to go to piano twice a week. Eventually, Laurie and I smuggled moth balls in every pocket hoping our moms would notice how we smelled when we came home from piano. Something did happen. We noticed Miss Masters gradually began to stink less or maybe we just got used to it.

Her other bad habit was that pointer and the metronome combo. The constant tick, tick of the metronome never stopped whether there was music or not. Her theory was you could be brainwashed to learn tempo. And with the pointer hitting you every time you hit a wrong key, it would instill finger memory kind of like muscle memory. It did not work for me. She also tried using the number matching note and finger method. Her new remedy added nothing but confusion and frustration to an already bleak situation.

Miss Masters had been teaching piano for 50 or 60 years. As long as the parents were willing to shell out the cost of lessons, she had the patience to whack away at students who had absolutely no desire or intention of learning to play the piano. She did seem to enjoy her fondness for whacking our fingers. I doubted she liked children especially those of us with no musical ability. After three agonizing years for both of us, she admitted that I was a lost cause—to my utter euphoric delight.

Mother held tight to her dream until she was completely exasperated, and her common sense forced her to lower her expectations. "Just learn to play for your own satisfaction," she pleaded. After three years of lessons and constant nagging me to practice, she acknowledged defeat. I was not the least bit interested. The recitals were further proof that I needed to continue my talent search. The competition and challenge of sports called my name much to Mother's dismay. Show me a baseball or a basketball hoop and my face lit up like a Christmas tree. Practice? No problem. I would shoot hoops until the cows came home.

She made one last admonishment. "Claire, someday you will want to play the piano. I hope you will come back to your music and keep an open mind about what you are now rejecting. Playing sports may be fun and even healthy, but it cannot take the place of music. I hope you will reconsider this foolish decision."

However strong my desire to please my adored mother, I was much too busy for piano. Just the thought of unending lessons, incessant hours of daily practice, the recitals—loomed before me as giants of boredom and wasted time. Also, just the thought of growing old with mean Miss Masters was too much for me. *Children should have rights.*

Chapter 6. Travis Wayne

Especially during the summer, my creative juices worked overtime on how to spend my days. As long as I stayed out of trouble and my parents weren't called to bail me out, I had free rein to explore my town. The local undertaker's boy was younger, a giant pain in my behind and a smart aleck but, as a last resort, he was usually around town looking for ways to have fun. We bickered like an old, mismatched married couple, but he was okay to pass time with. Trouble was, we were a whole lot alike; each of us was known as a know-it-all. He and his parents lived in an apartment above the funeral home so they could be on call 24 hours a day, 7 days a week. Travis Wayne felt confined and lonely; not many of his friends wanted to come to the funeral home—too creepy. I did not mind it. In fact, I found the place intriguing. Dead people weren't going to hurt you, and it was much more interesting than annoying Travis Wayne. One afternoon with temperatures soaring, we decided to play indoors. It was an ideal occasion to satisfy my curiosity about something that had fascinated me forever.

"Hey Travis, you promised to take me into the showroom. Let's do it today."

"You know better than that, Claire. It's pretty much off limits. Besides, we should at least wait until my parents are away on a funeral."

"Aw Travis, you wimp. You're just an ol' scaredy cat afraid to go in there."

"Am not. I've been in there lots of times. My parents said that it's not a place to play. Besides, there's nothing much to see."

But I would not be satisfied. "Yeah, but I want to. I won't make a mess, I promise."

Travis was totally exasperated but admitted when he was licked.

"Okay, Claire, but we'll have to make it fast. If we get caught, I won't see daylight for the rest of my life."

As we climbed the stairs, we passed the oversized door leading to the embalming room which reeked of formaldehyde. What a terrible smell. Travis Wayne said he hardly noticed it. It was just the aroma of home. What? How can anyone get used to a smell like that? Then Travis continued on a tirade of how bad the smells in a funeral home can be— just to impress me with how tough a little toot he was. He would use any means to impress no matter how gross or feeble the attempt. He had a story he couldn't wait to tell me.

"Shoot, Claire, you don't know nothing about what happens to dead people. Last year a couple got *fixated* in their garage, left the car running one winter day and nobody found them for four days. When they brought them in, Daddy said it was rotting flesh. We stuffed towels under the doors and windows, but it still stunk for weeks. Made Mother get sick and throw up. She couldn't even fix the lady's face and hair. Daddy and S. J. tried to do it. They didn't even have an open casket funeral. They practically had to close this place down. Mother and I went to stay with Gran for almost two weeks."

"Bet that was stinky. Don't you mean '*asphyxiated*'?"

I couldn't wait to correct him. At the top of the stairs, we reached a small landing with two settees and a couple of tables and lamps. It was cozy, to say the least, with no natural light, and the air was stale and stuffy. Travis Wayne led the way.

"Wait up. I'll make sure the coast is clear."

He stood still putting his finger to his mouth cautioning me with "ssh." There was no need for him to tell me to be quiet: he just liked to try to boss me around. To the right was the apartment where they lived. Travis immediately turned to his left and quickly opened the door, simultaneously flipping the light switch.

"See, Claire, It's a casket showroom. No big deal."

I did not agree. It was indeed a big—no giant—deal. Rows and rows of caskets in every color. Metal ones in pink, blue, silver and gray. Shiny inlaid woods with jewel-like brass hardware and handles. I saw a few plain vanilla, primitive-looking wood coffins that noticeably were the cheapest, way in the back practically hidden from view.

"Wow! There are tons of them. I love all the colors and the metal ones. They feel so cool."

I rose up all of a sudden after putting my face on the casket leaving a smear.

"What are those giant metal things?"

"Look what you just did. You left a greasy print." Travis took his shirttail rubbing frantically to get the spot clean.

Travis was annoyed. "Those 'metal things' are called vaults. You put the casket in them when you bury people. Don't you know anything? Now, can we get outta here?"

"No, not yet. Look at the puffy, silky material."

I ran over to softly stroke the soft lavender interior of one open gray model. "It's as soft as a pillow."

"Claire, don't touch it with your grimy mitts. Okay, you've seen it. Now let's go."

"No, I want to see how it feels. I want to get in."

"What? Are you nuts? You cannot get in the coffin. Get that crazy idea out of your head."

Before he finished his sentence, I was attempting to hoist myself.

"Come here Travis and help me."

"No!"

I continued to try to lift myself over the edge and then tried to jump in. It was no use. He might as well get it over before catastrophe struck. So finally he gave me a boost, up and in. I couldn't help myself—I was laughing hysterically.

"Wow, bet I'm the only live person ever to get in this thing. Do people test these out before they buy one?"

"No, Claire. They don't. The people who come in here are not here to climb in a casket. And yes you are the *only* person to ever get in that casket. Now can we go?"

It was the most fun Claire had had with Travis ever.

"Thanks, Travis. I owe you one. Oh, by the way, *habeas corpus delicti.*"

Huh? He just shook his head. He needed another friend.

Chapter 7. Marshall

I suppose most towns have an eccentric like Marshall although I've done no research to back up my claim. In reality, I believe he was a hoarder and loner. He just wanted to live in his own world to collect stuff and move it around on his property as he pleased. We liked to make up our stories, but there was nothing sinister about him and certainly not *To Kill a Mockingbird* Boo Radley type. Admittedly, he was anti-social which generally made most people nervous and caused a few to be even more intent on imposing themselves on him. If I walked to school, I had to pass his house twice since there was no alternate route. Naturally, my child's imagination went wild. He was that kind of strange man in a strange house so only a spooky story would do. I wondered who he was and what was going on inside his head and inside that house. Someone (likely a kid) with a rather nasty sense of humor nicknamed him "Skipper King of Thrones" and the name stuck.

At the beginning, I thought it all awfully comical. He seemed to me to be harmless, although he was foreboding. He gave off red flags that he was not the type to mess with. He went about his day not hurting anyone, and he seemed happy with his treasures. The problem was that he had one of the largest and most visible corner lots in the neighborhood—over an acre. He worked from daylight to dark to keep his yard well supplied with a variety of items. Yet, he was known for a particular commodity. His yard was covered in white porcelain thrones. There were dozens of potties of every shape and size. Every spring these bowls were transformed into planters proudly sprouting every color and variety of flower known to man. Inside the yard were old abandoned sections of iron fences and gates, terra cotta pots, old faded signs from Coca-Cola to Esso, Sinclair dinosaur, even Burma Shave. His passion was collecting. Whether in the boiling sun or freezing rain, his skinny, weathered brown body was seen, shirtless and barefoot, incessantly moving and constantly shifting items. We called it Skipper's Musical Chairs. He would shift his potties almost daily it seemed, making a meticulous circle, square or straight line depending on his whim, like soldiers in precise formation.

One day on the way to school, my dad pulled the truck over in front of his house to say hello. I was horrified. No one stopped to talk to Skipper. He did not like people. Curiosity seekers beware! He was what my mom referred to as anti-social. She also described the property as blight. But she insisted that, in spite of the visual nuisance, Marshall deserved to be treated with kindness. "Everyone should leave him alone," Mother advised. "He's not hurting anyone or causing any trouble although I suspect he is unstable."

My dad (always one to have his own ideas) had his own way even where Marshall was concerned. Most people were not threatened by my dad and felt comfortable around him. I guess most folks knew he just loved people. He did occasionally stop to talk to Marshall, but Marshall was unpredictable. That morning, Marshall was busy getting his treasures in what he considered to be the perfect order. He never acknowledged our presence, never stopped moving, and never looked up. He made a vigorous waving motion with his right hand for my dad to move on, still bent over and intent on the task before him.

"I'm busy. Can't talk, Chastain. Got some new stuff I need to put in."

Skipper was impatient and growing agitated. My dad obviously did not move rapidly enough.

Then he waved violently and yelled, "Get outta here!"

As I was surveying all this, I noticed the assortment of items. There was a rusty red kiddie pedal car, wheels intact but the steering wheel was missing. I saw piles of old tires and rims, wagon wheels rotting, old lawn mowers missing most of their parts and bicycles galore. Rusty and broken was the common denominator. There were several giant, handwritten "No Trespassing" signs posted throughout the yard. He did not tolerate any outsider on his property and had been known to fire warning gunshots. He was deadly serious about his collection and about his dislike of violators.

Efforts by the town to get rid of the eyesore were to no avail. Once a court order to clean up the property was enforced, he replaced whatever had been hauled away. His family refused to have *him* hauled away as many in our town voiced as the answer to the problem. Ultimately, Skipper's bizarre behavior and paraphernalia were accepted as part of the landscape of the town. It was pretty much accepted although unspoken that Skipper was not like the rest of us but harmless so let him be. His collecting had proven to be therapy, and the moving and shifting of his items each day gave him work and a reason to get out of bed. Those who were bothered by the visual pollution of it all had to rely on patience and tolerance until someone devised a creative way to get rid of the nuisance. I had decided that, in my limited experience, we were all weird in some way. His uniqueness was out in the open, so to speak. His choice to live in isolation with his junk as companionship did make him legendary however. As the years went by, I became increasingly aware of how someone developed that philosophy.

The destined sad day did come several years later. When we drove by his yard, the weeds practically covered the house. All the junk had been hauled away. Skipper was gone. The complaints by the public became too numerous, and he was difficult to manage. He did not stay on his medication and became increasingly withdrawn. The town was afraid of what they did not understand. Children had to walk by his property to and from school. His family hospitalized him for a few weeks to be "stabilized." In his absence, in the darkness, someone had violated Skipper by encroaching on his property, smashing and destroying every item they could get their hands on. That proved to be too much. He committed suicide.

For weeks, I carried the weight of crushing sadness that I felt for Skipper and for our town. In my child's mind, I felt that we had failed him. Surely we could have done something to help him. Maybe the townsfolk were genuinely concerned about the children. Perhaps they were focused on the eyesore his property presented. What about his service to this country? Didn't that count? He had served as a Merchant Marine during World War II and had been discharged to come home. After his duty in the Merchant Marines when he did return, he was a changed man. There would be no tranquil, peaceful life for him after his service.

He lived in that house and in our town for over twenty years. We never knew him; we didn't even refer to him by his proper name—just a stupid nickname that we thought was funny. But we judged him by what we saw, the effects of the illness of shame, mental illness. His horrors were his burden to carry until the end. Part of the human condition I suspected.

The house was bulldozed, and a new modern house was built. Strange what we become accustomed to. Call it progress but that wood box of a house looked as out of place to me (pardon my language) as teats on a boar hog, my dad liked to say. No matter how hard we tried to erase the past, the image of Skipper remained with me. I recognized he was a problem without a solution that ultimately he solved in the most distressing, sorrowful way. I did not have the answer. But I believed we all carried the burden of this outcome. Humanely, it was sad and devastatingly more complicated than just being rid of him.

Chapter 8. The Man
with the Plum Trees

I received the Christmas present of my dreams at age ten and spent most of the winter planning our tours around town. Would spring and summer ever get here? I had been accustomed to walking almost everywhere I wanted to go within downtown, but the idea of my own transportation was almost too overwhelming—WHEELS. It never entered my pea brain that the freedom of it all might be too much responsibility for me to handle. The electric blue Huffy came with all the bells and whistles I had specified including a push button horn and a basket on the handlebars installed by my dad. The privilege of riding this bike came with fine print, but predictably I pushed the geographical boundaries which made no sense to me. The part of town that held the most attraction was also the sector that was forbidden territory.

Up north of town, the houses were similar to those in the country. The lots were bigger, many had metal storage buildings and barns in the backyard, orchards and gardens and overgrown vacant lots with horses, chickens and goats. My mother had repeatedly warned me against riding my bike in the area. There was one house in particular that might as well have been lit up in neon. It drew me like a moth to a flame. The place that held the most fascination was the town's meanest man with the most prolific plum and peach orchard around—Old Man Grayson. During season, the trees were so heavy with fruit they looked as if they were going to *tump* over. Did he ever pick the fruit? It didn't appear so to me. He allowed most of it to ripen and then fall on the ground rotting. But one thing was for sure, it was *his* fruit, and no one else should have any of it. The challenge of Old Man Grayson and his forbidden fruit was too much to resist.

I made it my project that spring to enlist the help of my group to go on a preliminary expedition to check it out. Sherilyn, Laurie, and I headed out that Saturday knowing full well what we were up against. His reputation was well-known. His hatred of kids was in direct proportion to his love of his fruit. He had been known to tote a shotgun while he patrolled his property especially if he saw bicycles or heard kids. The trip was several miles by highway or longer taking the back way through the neighborhoods. After much consideration, we decided that the long way was the safest way, and we were least likely of being caught by our parents. The prospect of irritating the fruit farmer paled in comparison to our other overshadowing danger: the potential of being found out by our parents and having our wheels taken away. As we pedaled excitedly on our pilgrimage, the anticipation of our adventure proved almost as thrilling as the adventure itself. My heart was racing. The Huffy became incredibly heavy as if solid iron had been pumped into the tires. I could barely pedal the thing. I was shaking so violently that the front wheel started to vibrate uncontrollably. Although we would not stop and would not take any fruit, this reconnaissance was not without a plan. We needed to know the exact location of the most vulnerable fruit trees. Where were the doors of the house in relation to these trees? Was there an alley? How long did we need to make a getaway and not be spotted? Some of the streets did not go through and had small driveways or a garage in front. This mission would take planning and preparation. I had instructed my team on precisely what to observe in the space of a minute or two. Our strategy was to observe without being observed and to ride like the devil back home.

When we rounded the corner, the first thing I realized was that we desperately needed a Plan B. I saw him instantly. The shriveled-up old man in faded overalls was dwarfed by the large yard of rows of fruit trees. He was standing in the yard, hands on his hips and eyes blazing. Thank goodness, he was unarmed. "Whew." I said under my breath, "that was close." I spoke way too soon. When he spied the bicycle brigade, he transformed into a wound-up robot spun into action. He made a beeline for the back door. In seconds, he returned with a huge double-barrel shotgun! I was in the lead and sped forward trying to appear calm. I heard Laurie start to bawl.

"Be quiet, Laurie, and just pedal." At that moment, I wondered why she was one of our group.

He had the meanest, most piercing blue eyes I had ever seen. His dried-up brown face was as wrinkled as a piece of his dried fruit. All those years in the sun plus his disagreeable personality had taken its toll. Simultaneously, he raised his gun and ran across the yard towards us but specifically staring through me like an arrow piercing its target. His eyes met mine; we were already mentally dueling. He was ready to blast me away without blinking an eye. I would not be deterred. I was making a mental note of everything—the house, the front, side and back yards, alley, location of the windows and doors, the clothesline, shed, old car and small tractor. He fired two shots in the air. I experienced what "seeing your life pass before your eyes" meant. I felt lucky we were not hit, but luck had absolutely nothing to do with it. He did not aim for us—*yet!* I felt his eyes continue to burn a hole in my behind as we pedaled like the devil was in pursuit. But I vowed to return. *Someday.*

"Did you see those plums?" I practically screamed once we pedaled our bicycles into my driveway.

"You are stupid and crazy," said Sherilyn. "You might have gotten us killed."

I looked at the pale faces staring at me in disbelief. You would think we were from different planets. I was stimulated, excited and overwhelmed with my plans. My compadres were terrified, confused and positively done with me, maybe forever.

"Did you see those big juicy plums hanging over the alley? They were practically begging to be plucked." I continued my rant, but I was losing my audience.

One by one, my fading army peeled out of the driveway.

"You are a nut!" Sherilyn yelled over her shoulder. "I should tell my parents, but they would kill me. Don't ever ask me to help you again with one of your scatterbrained ideas. I don't even like plums!"

Laurie was still crying her eyes out, blubbering away. What a baby!

There were moments such as now that I didn't understand how and why we were friends. I began to suspect that the small voice in my head telling me this adventure was a bad idea had some merit. Some things I just insisted on learning for myself.

I was not sure what liking plums had to do with any of this, but I dare not say it. For certain, the challenge of stealing the plums was not remotely connected to my desire for plums. Not one of these girls ever mentioned our adventure, and certainly, no one intended a return visit. I had a plan that this quest would best be accomplished in the darkness of night. I had no idea of the unspeakable evil lurking behind the devil's curtain luring me in the form of a childish prank. It was more than I bargained for.

Over the next few weeks of summer, I was distracted by urgent and pressing matters of fun. *Ignorance is bliss*, so they say. Meanwhile, a critical life lesson darkened the horizon. Although it appeared a seemingly innocent distinction, I was about to learn the life-changing difference between stubbornness and perseverance. The town was horrified by the news. Old Man Grayson had done himself in. He had caught a dog on his property eating the fallen fruit. A neighbor's child had seen him angrily grab the dog by the hind legs and sling the dog repeatedly against one of the fruit trees and then throw the dog's limp and lifeless body into the alley. I was shaken to my core and forced to take a good look at my ten-year-old self. I was the leader of my group, and because of my stubbornness (my ego), I had insisted my friends follow me on this mindless adventure. In essence, I put my friends at risk needlessly—blinded by mule-headed ego. I promised myself to be aware of my actions and their potential effects as it concerns others.

Old Man Grayson was prosecuted and imprisoned but not for animal cruelty. The facts were much worse than anyone suspected. During the investigation for animal cruelty, investigators entered the house with a search warrant, but were not prepared for their discovery. Inside that house surrounded by the most luscious and fruit-laden trees, the man's crippled son was imprisoned. Once the door lock was broken and the authorities entered the house, he was discovered tied to a twin bed lying on a plastic mat. He had been locked in that small room starving, filthy and near death for months perhaps years. The smell from that room was so vile that it saturated the house and yard. The neighbors watched horrified as the emaciated boy was carried out on a stretcher. His bony arms hung limply, dangling off the cart as the attendants swaddled him like a baby in a cocoon of white sheet. Their faces were ashen, and tears flowed down their cheeks as they carried the child. These were grown men who were accustomed to seeing the worst yet were so visibly shaken they made no effort to hide their grief.

How did this happen in a town where everyone knows their neighbors and makes it their business to know their neighbors' business? This house of evil was beyond description and understanding. I learned the hard lesson that some people go beyond mean. People come in all shapes, sizes and forms. Some are basically evil. It is foolhardy not to accept the face of a person as presented to you. We all want to believe in the goodness of a person, but a person tells you who they are by their actions. I decided we would be wise to accept someone at face value. A case can be made that we were not nosy enough to know what Old Man Grayson was doing. Sure, maybe it is a fine line, but the experience was worthy of being noted as a life lesson of minding your own business versus watching out for those who cannot watch out for themselves.

There is a silver lining to this horror story. I saw firsthand how caring people effect change. Good things may magically happen but rarely. Someone steps to the forefront when it is not always easy. One of our families with three other children adopted the Grayson boy and cared for him giving him the therapy and love he needed so that he was given a chance at life. This is not to say everyone lived happily ever after. Everett would always require constant care. He would never be able to live alone. Because this family was willing to extend themselves beyond their own family, they made the lifetime sacrifice and commitment which was necessary. Otherwise, he would have been institutionalized for his entire life. He never would have experienced a family's love or the joy of living his life freely as part of a loving family. This extraordinary family deserved a special place: *Angel wings sighting.*

I had no inclination that I would be a senior in high school before my next visit to the orchard. Ten of us climbed into Janice Hayward's '57 Chevy convertible on a final spree.

"Where are we going?" I was curious and concerned.

"Oh, Claire, who cares. Quit worrying. We're going all over. This may be our last time together. Let's make a night of it." Sherilyn didn't want anything to ruin her evening.

She and Bobby were quite snuggly in the back seat. I was sitting on someone's lap who kept feeling my rear end, so I was not happy.

"I have to get back before 11:00 or my parents will send out the militia."

"Oh, Claire, you are impossible and a complete party pooper. Just relax," Janice scolded.

I was getting uncomfortable. At that moment, I looked up, and we were in the alley behind Old Man Grayson's orchard.

"Plums and peaches for everyone." Janice pulled up and stopped.

I was aghast. "How could you? This is a horrible, evil place. Get me out of here, or I'm walking!"

I was frantic. Janice squealed off leaving tire marks with loud shouts of glee from the car full of brainless teenagers. I tried to erase the memory of my first visit to that orchard so many years ago. That Saturday morning of our bicycle brigade was still as vivid as if it happened this morning as is the lesson learned.

Chapter 9. Family in Dire Straits

It was late May of 1955 and the last day of school. If I had known the sequence of events on this day would change our lives, I would have plotted a master scheme to be with my dad instead of sitting in a hot, boring fifth-grade classroom. He and I loved to drive out to Mother's old home place which took us out the farm-to-market road next to the railroad tracks. Mother had talked and planned for years about building her dream house on these 800+ acres of rolling grassland. The old wooden house where she was born still stood now weathered to a soft gray patina. She planned to use the barn wood in the new house in the den perhaps as a ceiling or as part of the fireplace surround. I kept my horse Latigo out here in one of the smaller pastures, so I knew this land by heart. It smelled so clean and fresh and felt like home out here. I loved the open fields covered in wildflowers and bluebonnets in the spring and sunflowers in the summer. Their big, fuzzy brown faces fringed in yellow shone with brilliant joy as they turned toward the blistering sun. It was the perfect place for our new house. I wondered: would this "dream house" ever be built?

Vagrants liked the shelter of the old vacant houses, so Dad made it a point to drive by to check on things. On this particular day, the arrival of a family into the dilapidated once white three-room shack was conspicuous. Not because they caused a disturbance but because the presence of a family like that in our town stuck out like the proverbial sore thumb. Most of the families here struggled somewhat economically, but this was poverty at its ugliest.

The old ramshackle house was easily seen on the outskirts of town next to the road and across from the railroad tracks. No one wanted to live that close to the train even if the house had been livable. Dad had mentioned that it was an awful eyesore and should be torn down. When he had driven by this afternoon, he saw that a family was living there. He commented that the house was so rundown to be hardly livable. He was appalled that someone would charge good money for a family to live in that place. But, he had to admit, this pitiful excuse for a dwelling was providing much-needed shelter, however primitive. There was no electricity. There was running water to the kitchen sink, but the bathroom was an outhouse. The porch had been screened in but now was so filled with rips and holes that it hung in huge swags providing no protection. The roof looked one strong blast of wind away from collapsing. The paint had long ago peeled away so that the bare, weathered and rotten wood showed through. There were small holes in the crumbling wood all the way to the interior of the house. The old rusty wire fence struggled to contain a yard full of knee-high weeds. An equally rusty, once-red rain barrel collected water for bathing and household use.

In a few days, Dad made it a point to go by the house; not because he was nosy, but because he was concerned and felt a strong responsibility to know what was going on in his town. As he turned off the main drag and across the railroad tracks, he saw three children walking along the side of the road. The ragtag group was led by a small girl followed by two even smaller boys. Their heads were all down as if they were looking for something in the weeds. Dad pulled his pickup to a stop and got out to see if they had lost something.

"No sir," said the girl. "We are looking for coke bottles. We need to take the bottles to the store to get some money."

"Well, said my dad, "let me see if I can help you find some. Y'all sure need to be careful on this road. People drive kind of fast, and you might get hit by a car."

At that point, the mother came out into the yard, and my dad went over to say hello.

"Yes, we just moved here, and my two older ones will go to school this year. We are the DeLaneys. My name is Ella. That's my daughter Libby, who is ten, and her brothers are six and four," she said.

Dad explained he was on the school board and would be happy to help get them enrolled and that he had a daughter Libby's age. Maybe she and Libby could get acquainted.

He offered, "If there is anything I can do to help you get settled, just holler. I am around town most all the time."

That evening at supper, he mentioned to us that he had stopped by to see the new family.

"Their daughter Libby is just about your age. We should go over now that school is out and make a new friend."

I was not excited or even slightly interested but, knowing my dad, I resigned myself that it would happen. I already had my friends—Sherilyn and Laurie—since before first grade. I had lost Ginny my best friend, so maybe Dad was right. Perhaps it would be fun to make a new friend. I didn't see me having a friend who lived on that side of town; I'd never known anyone who lived there.

We had no government agencies or welfare to take care of the needy. Our four churches—Baptist, Methodist, Church of Christ and First Christian Church—led the way to help anyone who needed it without question or judgment. In our town, you knew when a family was experiencing financial difficulty and they never had to ask for help. It was about pride. That Sunday Dad made sure that the ladies auxiliary were aware of the needs of the family.

"They need our help," said my dad, "but I need to make sure it is okay with the mother before we take some things over there."

That afternoon, Mom, Dad and I made our first visit. The kids were playing in the yard and excitedly ran up to the car.

"Hi, mister. Did you bring us some bottles?"

My dad smiled. "Not today. But we will get some next week."

The mother had heard the commotion and came out on the step. We all got out of the car and Dad introduced us. Libby stared at me and then scurried around the side of the house followed by her brothers. As we went inside, we saw there were two younger children. The youngest struggled to toddle. Seemingly unfazed, Dad explained the church wanted to welcome them and asked if it would be all right for some of the ladies to visit and bring a few things by.

"Why, yes, we would appreciate that." Libby's mother smiled.

After a few other pleasantries, we said good-bye. I hurriedly climbed into the front seat of our car between my parents. I needed them close. My mother was shaken, and her porcelain face was drained—now pasty white. "Oh, my, they are in dire straits. Those children are bony skeletons."

I kind of understood but did not want to visualize going hungry every day. I still wondered about something else that bothered me.

"Mother, Libby ran away when she met me. I don't think she likes me."

"I don't think that is why she ran away from you. She doesn't know you. You have to remember that she is a stranger here, and her family is going through some hard times. She might have been embarrassed. Think about how you would feel if you were in her place. You have to do all you can to befriend her. She needs a friend. Remember how you learned in Sunday school that we all must take care of each other and treat others like we want to be treated. If you don't remember anything else, daughter, remember to do that please. Also remember we never know what may happen. We might be in their place someday."

"Let's not go out to the home place today. I just want to go home." Mother shifted in her seat and folded the house plans in her lap. She had been working on those house plans for years. She had selected the exact spot where she wanted to build her dream house and talked about how nice it would be to live in the country. She spent her sleepless nights at the kitchen table drawing plans down to the smallest detail. So I wondered: what in the world were they waiting for? Was it merely a dream she had without hope of ever fulfilling it? I heard old people talk about stuff they planned to do but somehow never got around to doing much or any of it. Then they died or got sick and that was the end of the dream.

I did not say anything. Sadness and guilt overwhelmed me by what I had seen. Why did a family have to live that way? Further, why did I have to see it? I was upset and not in the mood to do anything but go home.

Chapter 10. Family Solution

The next week Dad went to the local café for early coffee as he had done for fifteen years. When he entered, he saw his usual group gathered at the counter bringing in the day. As he walked over to join them, the large door to the kitchen swung wide. He saw a small figure standing over the steaming hot water strainer basket of dishes. The small girl then reached with oversized rubber gloves flopping as she struggled to grasp the rack of heavy dishes, picking them up out of the boiling water and placing the rack on the dish drainer. The steam was so thick he scarcely made out the small figure. The strainer basket was almost the size of the small girl he recognized as Libby.

"Hank, I see you have a new dishwasher. Isn't she too young for that work?"

"Well, I know it. But her mother came in here with her the other day begging me to hire her. Said they needed the money bad for food. What was I supposed to do? She is only going to work here for a little while."

"Hank, we have to come up with another solution. She is too young and too small to work back there. She's going to get hurt."

The next week, Mother and the church ladies made their first visit to Libby's. The minute they took the cardboard box out of the car, Libby made a beeline out the back door banging the hanging-on-hinges screen door. The mother unpacked the canned food, some home-canned goods and a few clothes including some of my old clothes which no longer fit me. Mother and Libby's mom talked about getting the kids in school in September which was the most important thing to her. The woman had tears in her worn eyes and was grateful for everything and pleased they came by. My mother assured her that she would be back to visit again soon.

As I lay in bed and looked around my room, I thought about the family. My bed was a beautiful old mahogany spool bed with vanity to match. On the top of the vanity was my most treasured possession. The ceramic lamp was in the shape of a stunning young woman with hair in curls and wearing a huge blue ball gown and carrying a large white and gold fan. The triple mirror had side panels that folded to change positions so that you could see yourself from every angle. All had belonged to my mother when she was a girl. Beside my bed was a large Zenith radio almost as tall as I. At night, I tuned in stations as far away as New Orleans and Chicago. That radio connected and transported me to the unfathomable outside world and to radio drama. I listened spellbound to the gripping tales of *The Shadow*—"Who knows what evil lurks in the hearts of men?" "The Shadow knows."

The shiny hardwood floors glowed in the light from the living room and continued their way down a short, narrow hallway. Off the hall was a small bathroom we three shared. The hallway continued to my parents' room adjoining a small sleeping porch with a wall of windows that we opened in warm weather for cross ventilation. Even though we had no air conditioning and a couple of table fans, our house was airy and comfortable. Our large country kitchen was light and bright with a red Formica table and four chairs where we gathered for breakfast and generally every night for supper or games. Dad got up early and made my breakfast so that Mother had time to get ready for the day. From the kitchen, you could see the living room with the piano on one wall and a formal dining table in the corner. There was a large open-flame Dearborn gas heater where Dad and I had our ice cream on winter nights. Then off the living room was my room. These five rooms made a complete circle of the small house that I loved. We had three sets of French doors that shone like crystal. One set in the living room led to the outside porch, one off my parent's bedroom to the sun porch, and a set from the living room to my bedroom. There were two front doors which everyone thought strange. Mother said our house was a bungalow and that it was not uncommon to have two such doors. As I surveyed all this, I felt guilty. I had so much, and Libby had nothing. How does this happen? She was just a child and didn't she deserve as much as me? I was aware of the familiar smell of honeysuckle breeze bursting through the window that felt so cool and smelled so sweet. I was lucky. I wanted Libby and her family to feel what I felt—secure and taken care of. I understood we were not rich, but we had plenty to share.

That night, I overheard Mother and Dad talking in hushed tones. Dad was not happy. He had seen a small girl working as a dishwasher at the café. He was pretty sure it was Libby.

He told Mother, "I will not tolerate this. She is a child. The town must step up and provide for this family."

Mother was upset and agreed that we all had to do whatever was necessary. The next Monday, Libby lost her dishwashing job. Hank explained to Libby and her mother that he could get in trouble for hiring her and that she might get hurt or burned.

Over the summer, we made weekly trips to see the family to take them food and the basics. The churches took up the slack. Collections were taken to help people in need no matter the circumstances. Enough money was raised to feed the family and to buy shoes for all the children. Libby began to come around and say a few things to me. I liked to play with her and her brothers outside, and we laughed easily. We played tag and hide-n-seek and climbed the old sycamore tree. We were as free as birds and not concerned with reality and the cold harshness of life. I went from dreading the visits to looking forward to seeing Libby. She and I giggled and looked into each other's eyes and were happy just to be kids. Sometimes Dad would give us money for ice cream, and we headed to the drugstore. The journey of our friendship had begun. I fought against seeing her as a poor, ragged little girl who would probably move on and out of my life and began to look past her circumstances. The process of acceptance took its natural course. She was someone I liked as a person, loved and trusted as a friend and I treasured our moments together and didn't want to think about life without her. Instead of looking down on her as beneath me, I looked up and admired her.

To me, it seemed the natural next step for her to come to my house. My parents said they would think about it.

A few days later, Dad asked, "Claire, is your room picked up?"

What a question. He knew that I did not like my room any other way but perfect. I was beyond the moon that Libby was coming to stay with me. When we picked her up, she ran out carrying an old paper bag. I thought how strange and tried to imagine what she had inside that bag. That crumpled brown sack was her suitcase. Inside was a pair of my outgrown pajamas and a toothbrush. But the main thing I noticed was her smile. Her face beamed. She and I were so excited about our first time alone, that we could hardly contain ourselves. We couldn't look at each other without giggling.

On the way to my house, Libby whispered, "You are the best friend a girl could have."

When she walked in the living room, she stopped dead in her tracks, staring at just one thing. Instantly, she ran over to Mother's spinet. Her eyes glistened with joy and wonder. She approached it almost reverently as if afraid to touch it.

"It's okay you can touch it," I encouraged. "Mother doesn't mind. She wants me to learn to play, but I can play exactly one piece. I am not good at piano because I don't like to practice and I don't like Miss Masters. She's mean. I 've been taking music lessons for three long years."

She looked at me puzzled.

"Here, I'll show you." I placed my fingers on the home keys.

Libby wasn't convinced. "Are you sure your mother won't get mad?"

"I'm sure!"

Libby sat on the bench and put her fingers on the keys so that the keys softly played.

"Oh, that is so beautiful," she whispered. She sat there in a trance.

"Good, you can play anytime here. Mother does not mind. She says that a piano is meant to be played, not a piece of furniture to gather dust. Dad plays by ear and plays a fiddle while Mother plays the piano. She's a pianist and plays beautiful music."

We giggled and talked and promised our friendship would never die no matter what happened even if we got old. We took our friendship to the next level. We cut our fingers and mixed our oozing blood. We were blood sisters. Our bond was not to be broken.

Summer was almost over with the predictable return to school.

Libby needed clothes, and I had the remedy. That afternoon Libby and I played in my closet, trying on and prancing around like the magazine girls. She came away with three dresses, several blouses, two sweaters and two skirts.

The first day of school came so quickly. The calendar said September, but it felt like summer. We should still be playing and not confined to a stuffy classroom. Dad and I picked up Libby and her brother. Her mother was not feeling well that day, so Dad said there was no problem that he would enroll the children in school.

Even though I felt grown up in the sixth grade and had gone to school with most of my classmates, the first day was always scary. Libby and I walked into the classroom, and everyone stared. The teacher Mrs. Hammond introduced us and told us to find a seat. I looked over the group and saw my friends that I had gone to school with since first grade sitting in the back giggling and whispering.

"Let's sit in the front, Libby."

I waved at my friends and took my seat. Recess was chaos. My friends Sherilyn and Laurie were on the swings waiting. They did not say hello to Libby. They did say they liked her dress. I gasped. Oh, no, this is going to be trouble, I thought.

"Where exactly did you get that dress? Not in a store, I bet," Sherilyn sneered.

Libby eyed her carefully then shot back, "From my best friend."

They all looked knowingly at each other, rolled their eyes and shrugged. I shot them both a dirty look daring either one to say another cutting remark. Libby did not appear to be bothered. But I did not shake it off. I did not want her feelings to be hurt.

Later, I told her, "Once they get to know you, it will be all right."

Libby was nonchalant, "Don't worry. I'm used to it. They are just lucky to have nice things which means nothing to me. It's just clothes. My mother says most people don't know *it from shinola*. Besides I can take care of myself."

She was not nonchalant about her little brother however. She went on the playground to find him. He was sitting by himself on the bench watching the others play.

"Why aren't you swinging? You love to swing."

"Those boys wouldn't let me swing with them."

"Well, we'll see about that. You have as much right to swing as they do."

Libby went over to the swings, grabbed one and started pushing him in the swing.

"Does anyone mind if my brother swings here?" The pint-sized bullies were amazingly quiet. The silence was deafening as her heart pounded rushing blood to her eardrums.

"Good. I thought so. These swings are for everyone to have fun."

The first day of school came to an end, followed by another and another. Gradually Libby and her brother seemed to blend into the school. I was hopeful, but that optimism was short-lived. During the second week, some of the boys ganged up on Libby's brother on the playground. Libby saw it and sprang into action. Before the teacher broke it up, Libby was punching the boys who had tackled her brother. When the teacher separated the pack, there were two bloody noses, a torn pocket on Libby's blouse and four red faces—ranging from slightly rosy to Libby's ruby red. She was on fire mad! The teacher took her by the arm and escorted her directly into the principal's office. Soon my dad and mother appeared and took everyone home. Libby's mother was upset and crying. Mother and Dad were doing their best to calm her.

Even I recognized this was an omen. The children's playground rules did not change. It could be a cruel place. As long as Libby was around, the bullies were, of course, spineless. Libby had her own share of problems. Someone yelled "poor white trash" and threw a paper wad at her as she walked into the classroom. She just kept walking to her desk. This was not her first encounter with a loud mouth or a spitball. Childhood poverty is a heavy load. She had been in school for five years and had been the target of many hurtful vile names she did not repeat.

I had seen their caravans go through town and heard our nasty remarks. Cedar post cutters were the poorest of the poor. Libby's family lived for a year traveling from place to place while her stepfather cut cedar posts. They were nomads without homes who lived in small public cabins. They cut down cedar trees to make posts for barb wire fencing.

They cooked their meals on open fires and used outhouses. There was no electricity or heat. Their children sporadically attended school. They moved from place to place trying to find work. No self-respecting citizen wanted anything to do with them, and certainly they didn't want their children to be associated with the ne'er-do-wells. I saw it differently. These were hard-working people who struggled to provide for their families and did not deserve their rotten treatment. The underlying message: come to town and get your gasoline and your groceries and then move on. It was another opportunity to look down on another human being and feel superior—no respectability and therefore no kindness or understanding due. Libby saw through the meanness as pure ignorance. I saw it as well-respected citizens with wicked tongues and no sensitivity for the plight of their fellow man with no idea what it's like to *have nothing* and to *be nothing*. How could they know what *existing without* means? Unless of course, it happens to them. Even I saw the ugly truth. There was no doubt. Whatever someone's desperate circumstances, feel confident that it was their fault for their position in life. This was blatant prejudice running rampant.

Libby told me she had gotten into trouble in other schools. As the oldest child in her family, she was the protector. Her mother depended on her. She had years of experience dealing with mean kids, plus she had a strong motivator on her side. She loved school. No one and nothing would keep her from school. She did not want to fight but stood her ground when pushed. She admitted she allowed herself to be involved in way too many scuffles. But this was one Raggedy Ann that would not let them get to her. She was tough and getting tougher with each slam—wiser, older and stronger. She and her family were not accepted because they were different from other people. But then she reassured herself, being different is not always a bad thing. And she reasoned there are a lot of other people who are rejected because they are different for vastly different reasons. She believed it wasn't right, but she acknowledged that it was real and would never change no matter where she lived or what school she went to.

Her mother's words rang in her head, "Sometimes you just need to back away, words are just that, words. Remember what someone says does not make it true." Her mother was right. She tried to shrug off being laughed at and made fun of, being greeted by finger-pointing and whispers. She had learned to handle the personal slurs, but when they extended to her family, she did not shrug it off as easily. The third week of school, Libby's mother took her brother out of school. Libby's mother was adamant about one thing: her children would go to school. She had to figure out another way. I wondered what was going to happen, but I did not ask Libby, and she did not bring up the subject. If I had learned one thing about Libby, it was: don't pry. She will tell me when she is ready.

Something strange happened in the next few days. I was going down the hallway on my way to lunch when I saw Uncle Evan and Aunt Angela Callaghan in the principal's office. Angela and my mother were sisters. That's odd, I thought, because their kids are already out of school. Why would they be here? Oh well, I shrugged it off as none of my business. Another strange thing happened; Libby was not at lunch that day. I did not see her anywhere. Maybe she had gone home for lunch.

Four weeks into the school year, my parents called a family conference around the red Formica table. I suspected it was about Libby. Dad explained that Libby's mother was giving her children away for adoption. He had spent many hours contacting families that needed and wanted to adopt these children. To me, Dad seemed to know just about everyone not just in this county but all the counties around here and throughout Texas. I tried to swallow the lump in my throat. Not all these families lived here.

"Will Libby have to move away?" I asked, struggling to hold back the tears.

"No," my dad said reassuringly, "Libby is going to live with the Callaghans. But you must not talk about this to anyone. It's private, and you might hurt Libby and her family. There are still a lot of details to be worked out."

I was relieved that Libby would not have to move away and promised I would not tell anyone. But I was troubled and confused. Most of all, I was sad. The concept of a mother having to give up her children and children having to give up their mother and their family was too much for me to process. I thought, well, my own birth mother gave me up. But somehow the circumstances did not seem the same. It might have been painful for my own mother or it might not. I did not know how she felt about having a baby and giving the baby away. It all depended on how she felt about me. Maybe she didn't want me so giving me up for adoption was a relief for her. So the heart-wrenching pain that Libby and her family must endure was beyond my capability to understand.

"Claire, I am sure Libby will tell you tomorrow," my dad assured me.

That night, I tumbled over and over in my bed. I cried my eyes out. I tossed and turned and got on my knees. I prayed that God would take care of Libby, her mom and all her children. Nothing like this had ever happened. I was so sad and my heart so heavy that my chest ached. The tears would not stop. Mother and Dad heard the noise and came running. Dad tried his best to explain. Libby's mom wasn't able to provide for her children, and she loved them enough to provide new homes for them. My mother was crying now, too.

Mother hugged me tightly, "Claire, you have to understand that Libby's mother is making a big sacrifice—maybe the ultimate sacrifice that a mother can make. She is willing to give her children up so they can have good homes. This adjustment will take healing and prayer for all concerned." Mother was like that. She never once brushed off the monumental moments of life as insignificant or inconsequential. She was a person who felt deeply and profoundly for the other person.

Dad was straightforward showing no emotion. "There is no perfect solution, but she believes this is the right decision. She has agonized for months, long before the family moved here. It is the only way."

The vision of the DeLaneys was permanently seared in my heart, and their final insult was embedded in my brain.

Libby's family solution was dissolution.

Libby's mother moved in October to Tennessee to live with her friend Helene. The old shack was empty again, and it looked more lonely and pathetic than ever—abandoned. Libby had moved to her new home with the Callaghans. She did not mention her mother again, but she did tell everyone she liked her new family. Some of the kids were jealous and resentful of Libby's good fortune, and some were not interested one way or the other in the family's problems. There were some who extended a hand of friendship and understanding. Mostly there were whispers and giggles and talk about the poor shabby girl who had a bad temper whose family gave her away. Some in the town doubted she would last long in her new home. I marveled at the people who were supposed to be the grown-ups with their wagging tongues and judgmental attitudes about this family whom they knew nothing about as well as the cold indifference of my classmates. But my mother put it clearly in perspective. The children learn from what they see and hear. They are a product of what the parents instill at home. Some of the girls asked how she liked her new home as if she had merely changed houses.

She answered without comment, "It is fine."

The town continued to talk about the DeLaneys and how awful it was and criticize and attack the mother as irresponsible and careless. Why would she bring all those children into the world and not be able to care for them, blah, blah, blah. But the fact of the matter was: they knew nothing about the character and strength of resilience of Libby DeLaney. I recognized that Libby had her work cut out. She had to live in this town where her past was forever paraded down Main Street for all to see, somehow rise above it all and simultaneously adapt to her new home and find her own way in this world with head held high. This was quite a load to take on considering she was still shy of her eleventh birthday.

All her brothers and sisters were taken by families throughout the State and beyond. The Callaghans had grown children in college, so Libby basically was living as an only child. We continued our friendship as before. She seemed quieter, but she was careful not to show any weakness. Her tough outer shell remained intact. She was unwavering, but that was Libby—no nonsense. She hardly ever gave in to her feelings. She loved school and was dedicated to doing well in her studies. She never missed a step. If she was having difficulty adjusting to her new life without her family, was sad or confused, she hid it well. It was understood but unspoken between us. Libby was hurting. She shared when she was ready and not one second before. I respected that. She would talk about what she called "her innermost deep within the heart" if and when she was so inclined.

Christmas of 1955 was a big one for Libby. She got a new bicycle, new clothes, shoes and a red coat. But her new cowboy boots outshined everything. For the first time, the clothing was new, not hand-me-down, fit her, and belonged to her. During the Christmas break, I spent the night with her in her new room. Angela had taken her to the city to buy new furnishings for the room now all in purple and lavender. She had the most beautiful canopy bed I had ever seen. The curtains, bedspread and canopy were all in matching lavender chintz, and there was a small slipper chair in the corner. Libby glowed with pride and hope.

"I owe them so much," she said, "I have to make them proud of me. Besides, what am I supposed to do? Wallow around like a hog in a pen and feel sorry for myself? What's the point in making this worse than it has to be?" But somewhere down deep she buried the hurt and anguish she faced without her family. There would surely be a time of reckoning, and she chose to cope in her own way. The best way to overcome was to get over it.

"Claire, I know that God brought me to this town and brought you to me through your dad John Chastain. It all happened that hot summer day when he saw us on the side of the road. Don't you see, Claire, how you and I were destined to be? Can you believe it? We're cousins now."

We hugged each other, and neither one wanted to let go. Libby and I had been blessed to have the rarest of friendships that would endure through it all. Libby showed me the letter she had received from her mother written on her mother's fortieth birthday. It would be the last time she would ever hear from her. She died the following spring although it was many years before Libby would know her mother had passed away. Libby reverently unwrapped the letter from its purple velvet wrapper she had so lovingly packaged. Tears welled-up in Libby's eyes and she smiled as she handed me her beloved letter.

December 12, 1955

Dear One,

You are always in my thoughts and prayers. I hope you have settled in without too much difficulty for either you or the Callaghans into your new home. This change is one of many that you will face in life. My hope is that you know that I love you and want the best for you and all my children. I know this change comes at a terrible cost to us all. I also know you are a smart little girl and understand that hard times come to most of us. If you look around you will see tragedy and heartache, others with difficulties, so always be thankful. You have a good family that will take good care of you. You have been a big help to me and carried a load for your age. Don't be foolish to think that I have not always known that you were a special child not just because you are my child. You have a caring spirit. That is the way to live, my precious one. One day you will look back and realize. Your character is the most important thing. We have talked about this. It has not changed because you have a new family.

The Callaghans are such good people and can give you a good home and education. I know you will make the best of it. I have not talked to any of the families since the children were placed into their homes. It is better that way so they can adapt to their new homes without any more hurt. Dalton's family has been so good to me and helped me so much. I stayed with Helene until I was able to find work and now have my own small apartment. They have their own families and struggle to provide for them. I try to stay busy and work as much as I can.

I am grateful to John and Nella for finding families for all of you. If the Callaghans don't mind, would you send me a small school picture? You are a big girl now, 11. You just had another birthday. You do not have to call me Mother. You can just call me Ella.

Libby, I hope you remember always I love you.

Mother

"Do you mean to tell me, Katie Scarlett O'Hara that Tara that land doesn't mean anything to you? Why, land is the only thing in the world worth workin' for, worth fightin' for, worth dyin' for, because it is the only thing that lasts."
 -Gerald O'Hara
 Margaret Mitchell, *Gone with the Wind*

Chapter 11. The Callaghan Ranch

This was one of the largest and most well-known ranches around these parts. In Texas, a town is known for the ranches surrounding it, and the ranch is an integral part of our towns. The Callaghan Ranch was not the largest, but it had a reputation for being one of the best.

This land was rich in history. It had been the home of Indians, the Spaniards, settlers and pioneers. Stampedes of millions of Longhorn cattle from Mexico trailed and grazed it. Man hunted its game as the wildlife was plentiful and not difficult to kill. By the end of the 1800s, wildlife was beginning to disappear and, as the population grew with increasing pressure on the land, various species became scarce and then gone—buffalo first and then antelope. Grassland became increasingly over-grazed; trees and brush invaded the prairies choking the grassland. Raising livestock as a business was dismal. White-tailed deer which were once so prevalent were rare as were bears and panthers, prairie chickens and beaver. Water became scarce. Natural springs and streams dried up. Gullies and stream beds turned into ravines. Erosion became a familiar part of the landscape.

Gradual restoring of the prairie grasslands was slow and took many years. Oats, sweet clover, and Sudan were sown and irrigated. Fertile soil along the creeks was transformed into an isolated haven. Bluestem and Indian grass and hay formed native hay meadows. Alfalfa fields were planted. The Texas Game Commission put out antelope and deer. Small flocks of turkey were released. Migratory birds such as Bobwhite quail, mourning dove and duck became plentiful.

The long reclamation process of the abused and mismanaged grassland had begun. Choking brush was removed; native prairie grasses planted. Springs and streams flowed again as the original vegetation and wildlife began to be restored. Changes brought by drought and weather were uncontrollable, but there ought to be a sensible balance between man's use and his support of the natural resources and wildlife.

Evan and Angela Callaghan lived on 12,000 acres of prime ranch land where they raised registered Herefords. His great-grandparents had owned the land since the early 1800s, and he inherited the land from his parents. Evan had spent his entire life on the Ranch. As overseer, his main responsibility was to ensure that the Ranch was profitable. His job was multi-faceted and not always harmonious. He was the conservator of the natural resources of the Ranch—the land, water, grasses, and wildlife—which required that he continually educate himself on the raising of cattle and on the latest methods of conservation. The value of the Ranch was intricate and consisted of the natural resources and tremendous population of wildlife and the cattle business. Its value was complicated by man's use and demand. Thousands of wild creatures lived here such as birds and mammals, hawks, owls and snakes. Hunting and fishing flourished thanks to the fish and game such as white-tailed deer and antelope. There were birds native to the area—mockingbirds, meadowlarks, hawks and owls, roadrunners, scissor-tailed flycatchers. So-called nuisance wildlife such as raccoons, opossum, skunks and armadillos served their purpose. A coyote, wolf or bobcat would occasionally be seen and hiding in the brush and rocks were the predators, i.e., rattlesnakes and copperheads.

The natural and unaffected quality of the land was accentuated by its stark contrast to people. The land makes no pretext. Its inherent raw and honest nature attracts you like a magnet. Evan Callaghan had lived on this land since he was born. Twelve thousand acres was not anywhere close to the size of the famous King Ranch, but to an outsider, it seemed the size of Texas. You could drive (and certainly horseback ride) for hours and still be on Callaghan land. The sheer size of Libby's new home was almost as overwhelming as the enormous emotional adjustment being required of her. The Chastains and the Callaghans agreed that I should be with Libby at the Ranch until she felt at home with her new family. They felt that I could provide the emotional support and stability

Libby needed. Libby and I agreed and were thrilled at the prospect of living together as a family.

As we drove over the bumpy country roads, I slid my hand across the leather seat and felt Libby's hand clasp mine gently. This was a night to remember. I wanted to make sure Libby did not feel alone. Six miles from town, they turned off the county road onto a gravel road and made a slight turn towards a hill covered by a magnificent brick and stone ranch house. The front yard was a huge grassy knoll with two giant oaks and a four-car open garage. I immediately spied a basketball goal anchored on one side of the garage. Once inside, they entered a screened-in porch and mud room with storage bins for boots, shoes and hooks for coats. I heard the tap, tap, tap of nails on the hardwoods as Libby's first greeter to her new home appeared at the screen door.

"Hey boy, it's okay. We're home." Evan bent down to pet the magnificent black and tan German shepherd. "This is our best boy, Rowdy."

"Evan! How could you? I doubt Ian and Seth would appreciate that." Angela grinned teasingly. "You're a good boy." Angela reached down to stroke the dog. "Yes, he does take good care of us though," she admitted.

Evan motioned for the dog to sit. "It's okay Rowdy."

"Hi, Boy. You are a beauty." Libby bent down as the dog approached her slowly. "I hope we can become best friends." She stroked him softly.

"You'll get used to him being underfoot. He follows Evan everywhere. He's our shadow and takes his job pretty seriously. Watch out for him though. He sleeps in the hallway between the bedrooms. Ever since we got him as a puppy, he's taken on the job to protect and serve. He's our personal ranch police." Angela beamed. She obviously loved that dog as much as Evan.

As they led the way, large brown leather couches and chairs and a large television dominated the sprawling den. A magnificent open stone fireplace joined the den and kitchen. This comfortable room where the family gathered and watched an occasional television program or where visitors were entertained was large and inviting. Stacks of National Geographic and The Cattleman magazines were stacked on the coffee table. One wall was devoted to bookcase shelves holding books and family photos. It was a room that was comfortable, worn and slightly haphazard but inviting. There were four huge windows on the paneled wall. The scuffed and scratched hardwood floors proudly shined showing years of wear. This house reflected as all houses do. It was clearly a house accustomed to lots of people. The den opened into a massive kitchen with a table for eight. A food pantry and cabinets enclosed the room in a large U-shape. It was obviously well-organized and well-planned to serve a crowd or big family. Open shelves displayed jars of home-canned tomatoes, peaches, pickles and beans. A deep-set garden window full of plants stood watch over an oversized farm sink. There was a double refrigerator, and a dishwasher which was the first Libby had ever seen. In fact, she had seen maybe three refrigerators in her life. Her family never had a refrigerator, just old iceboxes that required a block of ice for cooling food. A free-standing black and white ceramic gas stove was prominent because of its beauty and as the hub of this work center.

The living room and dining room were larger than most houses Libby had ever lived in. An ebony baby grand seemed the perfect size because of the enormity of the room. Down the hall were four bedrooms and three bathrooms. Libby's room was diagonally across the hall from the Callaghans. Their grown sons' rooms were at the end of the hall and shared a bath. Libby's room had its own adjoining bath or as Angela was quick to point out, "en suite."

As Libby and I went into the bedroom, Angela followed. "We were planning to paint your room, but didn't know what colors you liked, so you and I will do that soon. I did buy you a new bed," as she pointed proudly to the canopy. "It's a-a beautiful room." Libby stuttered so awe-struck she was speechless.

"Be thinking of what you would like in your room. It will be fun to decorate." Angela smiled and said good night as she disappeared down the hallway.

Libby gave me a puzzled look. "Claire, will you help me? I'm not sure what she meant, but I know it will be lavender, my favorite color."

She and Libby didn't sleep that first night. We were excited about her new family and her new home. Libby had to be confused and overwhelmed, but I wanted her to know that people cared about her. "This place is unbelievable. It is so big and nice. You're going to have to learn your way around, and it is not going to be overnight. You might get lost, and no one would ever find you out here if you don't know where you're going."

I had meant well, but had not chosen my words with care, and she was not reassured. "I'm tired and not in the mood to think about all that. I'll just take each day as it comes. There is too much to think about. We'll probably have to get up early so let's call it good night. I'm so happy you are staying with me for a while. Thank you, Claire. You are the best friend—and cousin—a girl could have." She giggled.

Libby's transition to the Callaghans was strange enough. The added unknown of living on a ranch the size of a small state owned by your foster parents was beyond strange, it was mystical. "All this" she concluded to herself, "is unknown territory."

There was a glow in Libby's eyes that I had never seen. I realized that this night was a culmination of strangeness for Libby. Give up your family, Libby. Come with us now; we are your new family. It was hard to conceive how Libby would cope with all this change and insecurity. Libby had to make this adjustment on her own, but I would do everything possible to be with her every step of the way. Life with the Callaghans on the Ranch was Libby's key to happiness.

When Libby and I awoke the next morning, we learned that breakfast came early. Evan was out the door by 6:30 a.m. unless there was some reason to be earlier. As ranch manager, he was responsible for everything that happened within the confines of those 12,000 acres. The magnitude of his responsibility was too much for me to even begin to imagine. The Ranch was basically its own community, and we took the school bus with the other children on the Ranch. We liked being on a schedule and knowing exactly what was expected of us.

Libby understood the rules. We had talked about the previous meetings with the Callaghans as well as the visit the night of Libby's arrival while driving to the Ranch and later at home. The Callaghans were straightforward. They were hard-working and respected members of the community. Common sense dictated they would not tolerate a problem child. Their two sons were in college, and now, at age fifty, the Callaghans were stretched emotionally to cope with raising an eleven-year-old. It seemed obvious that an outsider such as Libby skated on thin ice, and she must be thinking they could turn her out as fast as they had taken her in. She could find herself back to life as she knew it or worse. Her family was nonexistent, so there was no going back. It was a *point of no return*. At best, she might be sent to an orphanage. She was familiar with the concept of tit for tat. The Callaghans had given her a home from the kindness of their hearts. In return, they had a right to expect a certain level of behavior—good grades, involvement in school activities, personal pride and respect. They were quick to add, "Libby, we are not giving you an ultimatum. There is no timetable for adjustment." Evan saw her puzzled look and tried to reassure her, "The arrangement we have is a commitment and hopefully will be permanent." But Libby's reputation had preceded her. There would be no fighting. There would be no calls from the principal requiring them to come to school to bail her out. They also made it clear they had not spoiled their two sons, and so the likelihood of Libby being the spoiled foster child was nada. She would have to earn her place in this family.

I heard Libby's sigh of relief that the Callaghans were mindful of the enormity of the adjustment and did not expect too much too soon and would be patient. Libby believed she was able to manage a gradual transition. Otherwise, traumatized would be added to Libby's already overloaded baggage.

Everyone worked here. We had assigned chores after our schoolwork was done and increasingly the duties would be more numerous and more complex. Callaghan orientation was precise and deliberate. We were not confused about our roles in this new environment, and we were actually relieved to understand what they expected.

Libby had been through a lot for her age and showed the world a tough outer shell, but the fact remained that she was still a young girl. She had to meet the demands of her new life and the challenge of life without her family. She had to be determined to do whatever necessary to cope with all the change, and the Callaghans seemed to be the type of people she could respect. But she confessed, how could she know until she knew them? They were strangers and she had to *build* a relationship with the Callaghans. She admitted her options were limited. Pretty harsh the way Libby put it—respect them or find another living arrangement. She had maybe four hours together with all sides being on best behavior. She knew nothing about them. I tried my best to reassure her.

"Libby, you need faith that everything will be all right. I know I'm not in your place, but I know Evan and Angela. You could not have picked two more loving people for parents. Trust me."

Our second night was a long one with no sleep and a lot of talk. Libby was slowly and painfully opening up to me. She confided that her mother's decision to give her away played over and over in her head. She second-guessed that decision constantly. She wanted to be hopeful and wanted to quit hurting. Yet she felt an uncontrollable urge to retreat to her previous life: her safe and familiar place. After a momentary lapse, she realized delusion could not ease her pain and might prolong it. She had made up her mind to focus on the present. I agreed with her that she could not afford the luxury of dwelling on the past. It would cause hurt. What good would come from aching and longing for her family that did not exist? Fantasy might bring temporary relief from reality, but it was a total waste. I did not want to sound cruel or unfeeling, but Libby had to begin the slow, painful process of moving forward. That part of her life was over. The decision had been made, and the plan for all the children's futures had been set in motion. Her job was to blend into the Callaghan family.

"Claire, I know you are right and I know I can do this. But I wonder if it will ever be any different for me. I just want to *feel* like I belong."

"Libby, your search for acceptance did not start with the Callaghans and probably won't end there. We all want to feel like we belong, but occasionally we all feel out of place and even rejected. But you have to give it a chance. Becoming a part of a family won't happen overnight."

Even I knew something about the feeling of being inadequate. But I was also learning about the negative effects of being negative. I wanted to encourage Libby to use every positive force she could muster to meet the challenges she faced and to turn negative thoughts and feelings into positive. But I also knew: *The most powerful motivators come from within.*

"Gosh, Claire, you never told me you had such deep thoughts. And I thought you were just another pretty face."

"Very funny. Now if we can just get you to think fluffy thoughts, we will have accomplished something."

I lost Libby on that one. "What in the world is that?"

"You know, go from deep retreat to a surface float. Go from deep survival mode to pure joy of living. There's something to be said about lightening your load whenever you can."

Libby was dumbfounded. Then we both looked at each other and laughed ourselves silly to tears.

"You know, Claire, you have a point. It's going to be hard, but I do need to change the way I think. I should thank my lucky stars. Mother made her decision out of love and hope for all of us for a better life. I can't disappoint everyone when she was so unselfish. Nothing is free. No matter the cost, I have to focus on the positive. I have been given the opportunity of a lifetime. My adjustment is small compared to my mother's sacrifice."

"I have no doubts about you, Libby, and your determination. We're kind of all in this together. Most of us have negative feelings about something that we can change. Not everyone is against you, but most people have no idea of the adjustment you have to make. Remember, you and I can accomplish anything together. You're not alone. We all have to find our place in the world." What an understatement. If I had only known…

Chapter 12. Country Girls

I spent more time on the Ranch than I did at home for the first six months after the Callaghans adopted Libby. Everyone concerned (especially Libby and me) felt that I should continue to be with Libby during the transition. Life on the Ranch was an unexpected delight; it was truly another world for both of us. Eyes and mind wide open every minute, every second so that we didn't miss a thing. We were in a constant state of astonishment. The stimulating newness kept us distracted from the magnitude of Libby's emotional adjustment. I couldn't believe how much I had missed by not experiencing ranch life. My aunt and uncle were ecstatic to finally get to know me and to share their way of life.

Libby confessed she was overwhelmed. "Can you believe it, Claire? How can I ever make up for lost time? I feel like I'm drowning in ignorance. I want to know everything about this place. If I weren't so scared, I'd give out a big Texas YEE-HA!"

I had a feeling that Libby knew her life would drastically change but had no idea what was facing her. She liked to talk about how she loved the country over town, but she never dreamed that she would someday live on a ranch. Her knowledge of ranches came from those she had seen on the big screen. She loved seeing the land and the cattle that grazed for miles uncluttered by man's intrusion in stark contrast to the land in Western movies which had been blown barren by hot winds and burned by brutal summers. The solitude and tranquility of ranch life beckoned both of us, and we became immersed in our new environment.

It was easy to be connected to the land. This new world dwarfed everything we had known before which now seemed microscopic and in a way insignificant. As I began to discover the vastness of the Ranch, I realized that before Libby came into my life, I had taken for granted the wonder of all the natural beauty that surrounded me as mere landscape. At least once a week, usually on Sundays after church, the Callaghans drove us around the Ranch so that we could get some idea of our surroundings. The concept of purpose was apparent. Everyone and everything had a reason for existence. The function and location of each physical structure was well-planned and specific. The natural resources, the wildlife, the livestock, and human beings functioned best in unison and in a delicate balance. This goal, though difficult to attain and maintain, was the essence of ranch management.

There were countless barns—all had specific uses. I saw hay barns, feed and cattle barns, storage barns and sheds for machinery and ranch implements, livestock barns for refuge from the weather, and for the care of calving, sick, injured, and weaning animals. Many of the barns were constructed of rock gathered from the Ranch landscape as were many of the feeding and water troughs located in strategic locations throughout. Everything was thought through logically for efficiency. The feed had to be delivered to the feeders. The feeders had to be located in proximity to the cattle but also near where the feed was stored. It was all a result of careful planning and organization. Livestock grazed in various pastures and meadows. Cattle guards were used instead of gates to eliminate the need for stopping to open and close gates. Efficiency. The name of the pasture was posted at the cattle guard. The Ranch was a business and, on a ranch of this size, there was no room for confusion. There was an assortment of pastures to control grazing, and certain pastures were set aside for either summer or winter use.

The horses were cutting horses ridden by the ranch hands primarily for working cattle. Prized Hereford cattle were raised and sold as the primary business of the Ranch, and Evan was president of the local cattle raisers' association. I was surrounded by wildlife no matter where I was. Even when I was in the yard, I saw deer, wild turkey and birds all native to the area. There were raccoons, jackrabbits and cotton-tails, and clear lakes with catfish, bass and crappie not to mention turtles sunning themselves on warm days. But there were also the predators. We learned to be on vigilant watch for rattlesnakes and copperheads. It could be deadly folly not to be alert. All the ranch workers carried emergency rattlesnake bite kits. Once you walked out of the house and away from the home telephone, the means of communication were walkie-talkies used by all the Ranch hands.

We took a picnic one Sunday to Rushing Falls. How could this natural phenomenon be smack dab in the middle of the Texas I thought I knew? The pure cool, rushing water fed by streams splashed over magnificent boulders and rocks forming a pool at the bottom four to five feet deep. A giant overhang of rocky ridge provided shade most of the day over the pond. A small cave beckoned with Native American hieroglyphics. Libby and I loved to go into the cool darkness to sit and listen to the falls. I thought of those who had been here before me. Relics such as fossils and arrowheads were still found here. Numerous wells, lakes, ponds and streams throughout the Ranch provided water and sanctuary for livestock and wildlife. Fishing was one of the most popular pastimes for the residents as well as visitors. The Ranch provided day leases for fishing and occasional hunters from the city.

The communal garden at the Ranch was our pride and joy. Everyone pitched in to work in the garden including the children, and we all enjoyed the bounty. The kids helped make the scarecrow and screamed with joy when he was at last perfect—stuffed to the top with just enough straw and outfitted with the perfect old faded plaid shirt. Once the soil was tilled, we helped plant, weed, and harvest. As we worked, Libby told me that her mother tried to have a garden, so small and primitive compared to this one. It had served its purpose and taught her to respect and care for the earth. This garden produced potatoes, beans, peas, okra, tomatoes and some melons and berries. Irrigation was prevalent on the Ranch, and it was necessary for the garden during our droughts and hot, dry summers.

In exchange for the long hours of hard work in weather that can be brutal, the workers received benefits in addition to their wages. They lived in houses rent-free. Their accident and health insurance was paid for. Much of their food was provided. A beef was butchered once a year. One of the ranch wives raised chickens, so we all had plenty of eggs. She also had several exquisite peacocks strutting throughout her yard bedazzling the countryside with color.

It took the labor and dedication of many to keep the Ranch viable. There were five other families on the Ranch. Leland, Harold and Vincent were pasture men who took care of the cattle and regularly monitored the livestock for disease or injury, calving, delivering feed to the troughs and feeders. They also checked and repaired fences and all the cattle guards, gates, and barns, so no item requiring maintenance was overlooked. Alvin took care of all the machinery and vehicles. He also hauled the cattle that were either bought or sold all over the country. Evan as owner, manager and operator was responsible for the overall operation of the Ranch and was in charge of the registered herd and show cattle to keep them in top condition. Angela kept the ranch books for final auditing by an accountant in the city who did the financial reports and filed the taxes. The cattle records were Evan's sole responsibility. He was a well-respected judge of cattle and was asked to purchase cattle for buyers all over the country. There was always building or repair going on; the Ranch had its own carpenter and builder. Building was varied and constant whether new barns, terraces, roads, bridges or dams. It was an intricate landscape of over 75 miles of road and 24 cattle guards and bridges.

Libby and I were fascinated by all these intricacies of ranch life. Thanks to her, I had discovered a new and invigorating side to life. On the weekends, Libby and I began to help out with odd jobs such as cleaning stalls and helping keep the tools and equipment clean and organized. Evan would occasionally ask us to go along with him to see the Ranch. I enjoyed those days more and more. He was looking forward to their help. "I am proud of my boys. Ian wants ranch life and Seth is a pilot and seems intent on entering the service after college." They both worked on the ranch in the summers baling hay and helping Leland and Vincent with the cattle.

One weekend, Ian and Seth called to say that they were coming home. Seth had bought a small airplane that they were flying to the Ranch. There was a makeshift runway on one of the level pastures, but the cattle had to be shooed away for the landing. Seth would flyover Friday afternoon so that we could get the runway ready. I was beyond excited. Evan, Angela, Libby and I were sitting in the car waiting and suddenly heard the small plane overhead. Evan got the last two stragglers off the path so Seth could land.

"That was a perfect landing son." yelled Evan. We all ran over as they opened the doors of the small two-seater. All I saw were white teeth. Those two were beaming, high on adrenalin. Seth got flying lessons for his sixteenth birthday against Angela's wishes and his feet hardly touched the ground since. Flying was his passion.

Seth beamed. "Now Dad, we have to build a hangar for the ol' gal."

"You are right son. If you will look over to the south, you will see I have already taped it off."

Angela frowned, "We had planned a barbecue for this weekend since some of your fraternity brothers are coming in tomorrow. I don't know how you'll have time to build a hangar." They all grinned.

"Mom, you worry too much," said Seth. "The Piper Cub will be fine tied down for the weekend. Who wants to go for a ride?" I couldn't wait. Evan went first, then Libby, and then it was my turn. I loved it. Even though the plane was so noisy all you could hear was the engine, the beauty of seeing the Ranch from above had me hooked. From the air, everything looked effortlessly organized with everyone and everything in its place and *peaceful*.

Angela begged off saying it was getting dark, and she had to get supper ready. "Mom, you have to go flying with me. You'll be surprised how much you like it." Seth cajoled.

"Okay, but later son. Everyone is starving. Let's go get supper ready, girls." Angela had her way of putting an end to a discussion.

The college boys stayed at the bunkhouse, and Evan spent the day Saturday taking them all over the Ranch. That night there was a barbecue feast, and all the families living on the Ranch were invited. We spent the day helping Angela make food and preparations for the party. We smoked six huge briskets, made potato salad and coleslaw, fruit salad, pies and cakes. We set up ten picnic tables and made gallons of iced tea. I had never seen so much food eaten by so many people while having so much fun. Laughter and conversation was lively and relaxed. This crowd had a common bond. They loved the land and the ranching way of life.

Libby and I spent the night mostly giggling and staring at all the good-looking guys. I whispered, "Ranch life isn't going to be bad at all."

"I agree, for sure, it does have its advantages," Libby grinned. "But, you know, Claire, I love it. I can't imagine ever leaving this place." She suddenly turned serious.

I chimed in. "This is another world and, thanks to you Libby, I'm getting to know my relatives. You know, I've never spent any real time out here. I might even get to know my cousins. I had no idea that Seth was such a good, good-looking pilot."

"Leave it to you, boy-crazy Claire, to notice your cousin's good looks."

I looked around Libby's room that had become so comfortable and her sanctuary. The small circle patchwork skirt that her mother had made for her now hung in a gold leaf glass frame. Angela had worked on the skirt for hours. She ironed and pressed until it formed a perfect fan shape and was ready to be professionally framed. Libby's Mother's red peep-toe pumps (survivors from the 40s) stood proudly in a shadow box on the top of the chest of drawers, the long, worn leather ankle straps tied meticulously in a bow. Angela had arranged the shoes one on top of another at an angle so perfectly they begged to dance again. There was one other item next to the red shoes. It was a marquetry lacquer music box that played Edelweiss. Libby had admired the box on a shopping trip, and Angela surprised her on Christmas. I smiled as I remembered that, when Libby picked it up to unwrap it, it started to play. And right on cue, we all laughed. Angela had said, "Well, so much for my big surprise for you, Libby." It held Libby's few precious treasures—a birthstone blue zircon ring her mother received on her eighteenth birthday and Libby's own birthstone ring the Callaghans gave her and a gold heart necklace from me.

Angela made few demands during school days. We kept our room clean and helped her with the meals, laundry and housework. She was kind and gentle but reserved. Slowly we began to feel at ease around each other. She did not seem that open or appear to be anxious to be close to us, so we assessed our boundaries carefully. She kept a close rein on her emotions. Her arm's length personal space reminded me of Libby's own reserved space. We took her cue and respected her restrictions. We did our chores and schoolwork, spent time with friends, and gradually learned how to create a life. Libby learned to make basic decisions and how to voice her choices and preferences—things that may seem so natural but nevertheless were foreign to her. We made a couple of shopping trips to get school clothes and to furnish her room. On our first trip, Evan took us to a western store and bought us boots. I selected a pair of tan rough-outs with a walking heel. Those boots fit me like I was born in them. Other than the boots, I found shopping exhausting with too many choices and too many decisions. The Ranch definitely had me distracted.

Evan was much easier to talk to than Angela and fun. He had tireless patience and was eager to answer our endless questions about the Ranch. Not only did he not get annoyed, but he also seemed to welcome our fascination with our new surroundings. His love and passion for the Ranch was contagious. It was hard to explain, but I felt at home here and at peace. I liked the solitude, appreciated the land and the wildlife, and I was captivated when Evan talked about the challenge of using and enjoying the land but not depleting it. I liked and understood the moral obligation to those who came after. The land and its natural resources were to be valued and respected. I loved living on the Ranch—the self-sufficiency, independence, sense of community.

Libby began to feel she belonged and could be an equal. Here you were judged by your production and contribution, not by some frivolous measurement of how you looked, how much money you had, or the clothes you wore. She once said to me, "The land is alive and, much like a person gives and gives even though abused and still provides—up to a point. Then the land can give no more." Her analogy came from her experience and made perfect sense.

People commented on how well Libby was adjusting. Then three months after her arrival, the emotional upheaval took its toll. At breakfast one morning, Angela asked her if she remembered the night before. We both looked up from our breakfast. What was she talking about? Libby assured her that she did not remember.

"Well, it was pretty frightening." Angela continued. She sounded annoyed, or maybe she was bewildered. "We found you in the yard wandering around at two in the morning." She had heard Rowdy going nuts barking. Apparently, Libby went to the bathroom and then out the front door with Rowdy following. They thought they had awoken her and then led her back to our room. I did not recall anything either which was frightening. I didn't even hear Rowdy barking.

"Have you ever had this problem before?" she asked.

"No, ma'am." Libby was confused and embarrassed.

"Well, I hope it doesn't happen again. It's alarming. We don't want you to get hurt. I'll make an appointment with the doctor so you can get a checkup. We need to do that anyway."

The next week Libby had her first medical checkup at the age of eleven. The doctor found nothing unusual except for a slight heart murmur. He attributed the sleepwalking to her emotional adjustment and seemed confident that it would subside. It did happen again the next year, and then the sleepwalking stopped as abruptly as it had begun and life assumed its routine.

The Ranch was not all work. In fact, it was a lot of fun and offered a variety of ways to entertain and enjoy various pastimes. We quickly learned that the Callaghans' generosity was boundless. They made it clear that the Ranch was a place to be shared. We were encouraged to invite friends to visit, to have parties, dances, and hayrides. The hardwood floor in the enormous living room was as perfect as any gymnasium for our sock hops. The music was loud and nonstop as the big old Harman Kardon boomed through unlimited stacks of 45s and 33 1/3s of songs by Chuck Berry, the Everlys, Fats Domino, The Platters, Elvis and Patsy Cline. The simple menu of burgers and soft drinks was perfect. Angela loved having kids around. The one thing she asked was that we help her prepare for the party and clean up afterward.

Entertaining kids on the Ranch was nothing new. Ian and Seth had grown up here, and so had many of their friends. Evan and Angela delighted in seeing "young folks" at the Ranch once again. I was not alone in hog heaven. The activity, laughter and energy brought new life to them. The Ranch had a pit used for cooking and a protected area for bonfires. Evan or one of the ranch hands drove the truck pulling a trailer loaded with hay (that I had helped load) which incidentally took exactly twenty-four bales. Evan built a fire for roasting hot dogs and s'mores. We sang our silly songs and laughed about how stupid we sounded and played games or told ghost stories. Libby was often the butt of the jokes because she made herself an easy target. It was her way of gaining attention. I had not learned and did not show any signs of developing the fine points of restraint and sophistication. I, too, was not afraid of being laughed at if I was making a joke or trying to make people laugh. I learned that a little self-deprecation went a long way. Libby was learning social skills for the first time. Her tough outer shell softened and she learned her street smarts worked in some situations and in others was a total liability.

Libby earned the title as "Little Queenie" because of the fabulous parties and she was popular with our peers. She learned to enjoy being the center of attention and began to shed her self-consciousness. We had horseback riding, barbecues, picnics and slumber parties. I felt at home. Evan and Angela were pleased that Libby liked to have friends, made good grades and was a hard worker.

Her relationship with the Callaghans was based on respect. But she confided to me that it was less complicated if she kept her feelings to herself. She did not want to reveal any sign of weakness or reflect signs that she was having difficulty managing her transition. Friends of the Callaghans marveled at how happy and well-adjusted Libby was. There was a price to pay for her hiding her emotions. Yet it was a habit she couldn't seem to break. She continued to perfect her acting skills. Libby and I agreed: there are times you *need* to pretend. If you believe everything will be okay, karma will work as a positive force.

Libby and I talked about the one idea that she could not get out of her brain. This Ranch could provide so much for other kids like her. She had a dream about the Ranch that other kids could enjoy the Ranch experience during the summers. She was reluctant to mention her idea to Evan and Angela. After all, she was new to the family. They might think she was being pushy. She desperately wanted other underprivileged kids to know the joys as well as the work ethic that is a huge part of ranching.

"Claire, I'm bursting. Do you think we should tell your mother and dad about this idea?"

My dad was enthusiastic. "Oh my goodness, Libby, that is a fantastic idea. You have to talk to Evan and Angela. Trust me, they will like it. The reason they might not do it right away is because they are so busy and short-handed." John Chastain and Nella were glowing.

I smiled in agreement. "Libby, you are so smart and always thinking about how to share. I love you for that. Don't ever change. Now all you have to do is get up your nerve and talk to the Callaghans."

I liked the sound of it—Camp Callaghan Kids. "You better hurry and get this plan off the ground, or we'll be too old and creepy to be camp counselors."

"Yeah, we might be too old, but it's for sure we'll still be tenderfoots. We don't know diddly about the Ranch. We need keepers ourselves." Libby was so honest she was annoying sometimes.

Chapter 13. Snake in the Grass

A warm, clear day in March promised that winter was on its way out. And if that wasn't enough to celebrate, we had two weeks of no school. I was in the ninth grade spending spring break on the Ranch with Libby. Evan asked if Libby and I would like to join him on a pasture check.

"Wait. I just need to get my boots on." I yelled. That was one rule you never broke. Boots were worn for several reasons, but the primary one was for protection.

Rowdy stood waiting at the door, but Evan said no. "No boy. You're not going today. Stay here with Mom."

As we drove along, I commented, "What a gorgeous sunny day. I'm so happy for spring. Where are we going?"

"You'll see." said Evan, "I want to take advantage of the day and see how the Gilroy pastures are coming along." We headed further out than usual, and Evan made it clear, "You two have never seen this part of the Ranch. It's much denser with brush, and we've been clearing it for pasture."

He stopped the pickup and, as we got out, he cautioned, "Watch for snakes. They'll be coming out now."

We walked for several minutes and saw piles and piles of brush which had been bulldozed. "This land has been unused for several years. It will take a long while to get it back." He explained the painstaking process of reclaiming the land once the brush takes over. Just as he finished his sentence, from behind him, I heard the sound and saw the coil. "Don't move." At that instant, the rattler made its strike. It was too late for Evan. The snake had bitten him and then slid off through the tall grass. I had never seen any creature move so fast. Evan sat down shaken. Libby got his boot off. The snake bite was just above the top of his boot almost as if the snake had radar.

Simultaneously he grabbed his walkie-talkie to call Leland and looked at me eyes blazing, "Claire, I've got to cut this. Go get the kit out of my truck." I heard him on the walkie-talkie, "Leland, rattler got me. I'm in the Gilroy pasture. Gotta get to the doctor."

Leland's answer was short. "I'll call the doctor. I'm on my way. You know you gotta keep your heart rate down to try and keep that poison crap localized."

When I got back to Evan, he took the kit. His leg was already red and oozing. He had made the preliminary cut and applied the pump to get the venom out of the cut. Then Libby helped as he applied the tourniquet. I was in shock and terrified. I did not know what to do. I prayed for Evan. "Please hurry, Leland," echoed over and over in my brain. Then I heard a car. Leland and Vincent moved smoothly and quickly. They checked the wound and then laid Evan in the back seat. Leland had called the doctor, but the doctor had said to get Evan to the hospital. Time was critical when bitten by a rattler. Evan could die. He could lose his leg. At the very least, it was going to be a long healing process.

You never know how valuable a commodity can be until you have to have it. People were paid good money to hunt and kill rattlesnakes around here. The town looked forward to our annual rattlesnake hunt for months. The snakes that were caught were brought to town and placed in a large pit. Wranglers effortlessly handled and milked the snakes for their venom to make anti-venom. The festival atmosphere was foreign to me. Yes, it was a good thing to get the venom, but I did not want to see it all. One rattlesnake hunt was enough for me. All those poisonous killers slithering around in that pit just screamed nightmares. Depends on your perspective. Now when we needed it the most, the real nightmare would have been if we couldn't get the anti-venom. Our family faced our own real terrifying nightmare of what would become of our beloved Evan.

Cowboy and the Twilight Sky

He sits high in the saddle a dark silhouette
Against an azure blue sky cowboy and his horse a perfect duet
A painted swirl of corals and gray and azure blue,
Painted in time by nature's hues.
Lone figure in symmetry with nature's backdrop
Posed with perfection not duplicated with studio prop.
He rides in graceful precision without hesitation or care
Creating beauty and awe, breathtaking so unaware
Of the magnitude of his ride, a painted vista of inspiration
Across the horizon with purpose toward his destination.
They ride as one strong and sure to prevail
And linger not until they reach the end of the trail.
I gaze with wonder as he disappears from sight
The lone cowboy high in the saddle against an azure blue sky at twilight.

Evan was in the hospital for several weeks. His leg swelled to twice its size. He had fever and convulsions. The leg showed signs of rotting tissue and turned every color in the rainbow—red, purple, green, black. There was a chance the leg would be amputated. It took several skin grafts, but eventually, the leg showed signs of healing and new tissue. The doctor was hopeful because of the fast treatment however primitive. Evan was on the road to recovery. Rowdy laid by Evan's leather chair each day until Evan returned home. It had been a blessing that Evan did not take the dog with us that fateful day. He probably would have been snake bit also. I realized how deeply we cared for and depended on Evan. Angela and Libby stayed at the hospital the first week, and Ian and Seth came home. It was truly a family affair. They visited their dad, helped on the Ranch and took care of Angela.

I stayed with Libby at the hospital. Then, on the second night, Ian put his arms around Libby and assured her, "Libby, Dad is going to get over this, but it may take some time. You were a big help, and I'm so glad you and Claire were with him. This family is lucky to have you, and we owe you, kid." I saw that Libby felt she was beginning to earn her place in the family.

The storm of feelings held at bay for so long took over and tears flowed. I felt the love and devotion these people had for each other. How fortunate that Elizabeth (Libby) Callaghan was to be one of the Callaghans.

The boys were on spring break. This was Ian's last year of college. Seth wanted to join the service and fly helicopters. They worked on the Piper Cub's hangar in their spare time, and it was beginning to take shape. It was a simple metal structure to provide basic protection from the weather. Evan had not returned to full-time ranch work but was eager to supervise and give the boys some moral support and tips when they needed it. They showed amazing building skills which was not surprising. Evan and his sons helped build many of the Ranch barns. We all helped paint the hangar bright white and stepped back to admire our work. "That looks great! It needs one finishing touch, though." We were not done. Seth insisted it would not be complete without a State of Texas flag which he promptly painted on the slanted roof. Seth grinned. "Now the only thing missing is the ol' airplane. Trust me; I will take care of that soon."

I had enjoyed getting to know Ian and Seth. They were fun and easy to be around. They treated Libby and me like their younger sisters— teasing yet protective. I had recently started to date, and admittedly I was pretty awkward around the boys. I didn't enjoy that feeling nor did I plan on making it permanent. I welcomed any opportunity to "practice" being in the company of males. Unlike me, Libby had few distractions in the boy department. Seth was definitely exciting and seemed to always have something going on. He liked and attracted pretty girls. He had recently broken up with a girl and joked that he was moving on up to bigger and better. Well, he wasn't kidding. The next big news bomb he dropped was when he phoned Angela that he was flying in with the next Miss Texas. That Friday, he buzzed the house, and off we went to shoo the cows grazing on the runway.

Libby was nervous and not that excited about the prospects of this day. The beauty queen was staying with us in the same room. In my mind, I saw the headline that Libby and I would make in the local Gazette—"Local hayseed duo bedazzles state beauty queen." What was he thinking? Seth, you owe us one. Little green monster coming out, I guess.

As the want-to-be Miss Texas opened the door of the small plane to get out, Libby rolled her eyes. I crossed my fingers. Make her talented and not too hot in the looks department. Dreaming is enjoyable but not reliable. I noticed she was top heavy curvy, blonde and, of course, pretty in that order.

"Cassandra, want you to meet my mom Angela and this is Libby and Claire." Seth beamed as he put his arm around her waist and kissed his mom. Cassandra flashed perfect teeth and Libby flashed back.

I extended my right hand, "It's nice to meet 'cha Ca-SAND-dra."

"It's Ca-SOND-dra, hon."

"Sorry." I struggled to sound sincere.

"That's okay hon. A lot of people don't pronounce it correctly." I couldn't believe it. As she corrected me, her smile got bigger and wider as if every tooth in her head was vying for attention.

I thought twice about correcting her that my name was Claire, not hon.

It was going to be a l-o-n-g weekend.

We loaded her *two* bags into the car and Seth commented that Cassandra would compete in the Miss Texas pageant in two weeks and was an opera singer. "Yeah, I bet. But can she carry a tune?" I thought. Nasty Claire, I scolded. She and Seth met in animal husbandry class and had been dating for about two months. Her dad was a doctor in the city, and she had several horses and wanted to be a veterinarian. She couldn't wait to go horseback riding on the Ranch. Libby politely helped carry her bags and showed her to the room. Then she was on her own.

The next morning, we got up our usual time and got dressed, boots, jeans, shirt. The beauty queen was still primping, intent on every eyelash being coated with multiple coats of mascara, then separating each tiny lash with a straight pin, not near done.

Libby and I gave each other the eye that we needed to vacate the premises and leave her to it. "C'mon Claire, let's go help Angela get breakfast ready. Take your time, CaSONDdra. We're not on a tight schedule around here."

"Okay, hon. You two will learn it takes longer to put yourself together as you get older and particular about how you look in public." Ca-SOND-dra beauty pageant queen advisor. Much longer when you wear two pounds of pancake makeup, said me to myself.

"Yeah, well, that's what I like about living on a ranch. The cows and horses don't know if you are 'put together' or not. See ya." Libby was out the door leaving me with the beauty queen in a room filled with spray net so thick you could cut it with a knife.

I was my own judge, and Miss Cassandra was not making points with me. She merely reinforced my theory that most beautiful girls are shallow and stuck on themselves and not worth my time. So much for being beautiful on the inside. I was still searching for that one beautiful being that blew my theory to smithereens. She was after Seth. I figured he might do much better and hoped he was smart enough to see through her. If I chose someone to look up to, I definitely would aim higher than plastic wind-up doll baby. Careful Claire. I wanted to respond to her putdown, but thought, why bother. But Miss Cassandra was not finished with me yet. "Oh, wait before you go. Would you be a dear and help me. This darn bra is so hard to hook," as she leaned over to stuff all her stuff in the tiny bra.

"Sure." I'm just here to serve, under my breath, and out the door I flew. I was going to give Libby a piece of my very small, very perturbed mind.

Seth and Cassandra spent the day riding and then fishing and then whatever. We had a cookout, watched the sun go down and watched some television. Libby and I were on Cassandra Overload and needed breathing space. I went to our room to read and was asleep when Cassandra came in. Thankfully they left after breakfast on Sunday. As Seth tipped his wings to us on the ground, Libby smiled bigger than she had all weekend.

"Hey, Claire. Maybe we should watch the pageant. Might be fun to see if she trips and smears her painted face."

Ian was getting ready to graduate and was anxious to return to the Ranch. He and Evan had planned to open new pastures and grazing land, so there was a lot of work. Evan and Angela hoped to take a trip or two. Seth was entering Officer Candidate School. In a couple of years, Libby and I would be college bound. After much discussion, we agreed to go to the state college just like the Callaghans and the Chastains. Libby held on to her lifelong dream of being a teacher. There was no doubt in my mind. I had always known I would be a country lawyer just like my dad. My distraction had long since come and gone: a boy who once who tempted me to take a different path. I stubbornly resisted falling for him to the point of no return and repeatedly resisted changing that position. It wasn't easy.

Chapter 14. The Baby Bird

I was obsessed, practicing to be a teenager. The turquoise 1956 T-Bird teased and taunted from behind the giant plate glass windows of the Simone showroom. The shiny Bird took on a life of its own and, although unreachable and untouchable, it beckoned me into forbidden territory. My dad bought his pickup trucks from Simone. Just to keep me quiet, he begrudgingly took me with him to get his newest truck. Since that day two months ago, I had made the long trip every week on my bicycle to visit my new hypnotic friend. How could any car be so dreamy? It had what my dad called a continental kit, portholes in the hardtop that was removable and a convertible top. What else could any girl want? I begged my dad to buy that car. He peered over the top of his glasses and shook his head disapprovingly. He wasn't accustomed to my being so outlandish, and he didn't intend to establish a family precedent. He refused to tolerate such foolishness even from his pre-teen. And then he laughed out loud and stated the obvious. "You're twelve without a driver's license. What would you possibly do with a car, especially a car like that?"

"You could put it away for me until I'm old enough to drive. It won't be that long."

"I have a better idea. When you are old enough to drive, go to work and buy it for yourself. You have no idea how expensive that car is."

"But Dad they won't have this car by then. I want this car more than anything in the world. Look at it. Maybe you could get it for Mother and then I would drive it when I'm old enough."

"No, Claire. I've heard enough about this car. It's not in our budget and besides your Mother doesn't need a car. She's happy with the car she has."

Never argue with your dad, especially when he's a lawyer—you'll always lose, and you can get in big trouble. I was smart enough to shut up and accept defeat.

This was not my first T-bird experience. I instantly spotted the first one in 1955 when they first appeared in the marketplace. The banker drove one around town for all to see and then handed it off to his daughter when she went away to college. I couldn't get over that. My parents would never *give* me a car and certainly not *that* car. I was pretty spoiled but far short of sporting around in an expensive two-seater (albeit an American one) when I was eighteen. I tucked away deep in my subconscious the vision of me and that car as foolish and far-fetched. Best to set my sights on worthwhile and attainable.

But the Simones were intent on continuing my fantasy. They had to show off the latest model, the 1956. It was even dreamier than the 1955. I noticed the sleek little Bird the first week it took over the plate glass window. And that color was my favorite, so I surrounded myself with it. I had clothes and jewelry that color and my new bedspread was a shade lighter of aqua. I plotted that if I couldn't have the car, at least I could visit it. In my twelve-year-old-brain that made perfect sense and kept me preoccupied and prolonged my fanatical obsession.

I had not experienced such a preoccupation or close connection to any car before or since. In the 50s and 60s, cars took on a new dimension propelling us out of the war years of mostly boring and practical into the space age of stylistic design. I was not unusual for a kid that I identified most vehicles as we traveled along the highway. Cars were individualized with prominent characteristics. Tailfins on a Chevy or Buick were pronounced and distinctly different from those on a Ford. Grills and rear ends had their own uniquely identifiable differences. It did not take a rocket scientist to know one from another. It wasn't so much that I longed for these cars; they were, well, interesting and closely akin to rolling works of art. I loved the beautiful bright colors and the gaudiness of chrome from end to end. Polished and shiny they took your breath away. And they were *big*. We loved cars and took pride in recognizing the make, model and, if you were knowledgeable, the year, and all the variances and nuances of a special version. It was a fun pastime impressing your peers with knowledge of even the slightest variations that set you apart as an expert. It was a lot more fun than filling your head with usable information such as your schoolwork. Cars were fun and exciting again and much more than transportation. Cars were a significant part of the era and our young lives.

The Baby Bird was special for another reason: it led me straight to the world of a charmer rapscallion. But I still refused to make the connection. Okay, so I'm not the brightest star in the galaxy. I can focus on one thing, and this car had me transfixed. As it turned out, the car and the guy had a lot in common as did their effect on me. *Enchanted.*

Chapter 15. Fast Eddie Ray

His reputation as the wildest, most exciting boy in our town added to his mystery. I heard all about him and even had a dream about him. He was older and, as I visualized him, a man of the world. I didn't stalk him, but I did keep up with his comings and goings in our town. He like me was a street kid. I tried to make our paths cross but, as hard as I tried, so far I had missed the mark. The obvious vehicle leading to Eddie Ray's path went way beyond my limited scheming ability. I heard some of the older girls talk about him in hushed tones. He was known as a heartbreaker.

His dad owned the local Simone Ford dealership, so it was no surprise that he was all about cars. Al at the parts counter used him to shuttle parts to the mechanics. From the age of six, his playground was the service department with the mechanics as his babysitters. Since his dad owned the dealership and his mother wrote and signed the mechanics' checks, they had few options. Their job was to take care of Eddie Ray. He was the shining star in the Simone world and a spoiled brat. He terrorized the town with another brat—the son of the owner of the feed store. He and Eddie Ray spent the day running willy-nilly between the feed store hayloft and the dealership. Their bad habits and lack of supervision caught the attention of the local barrel-chested sheriff. He made it a point to impress them, "Don't let me catch you doing anything that I have to take you to jail." That ultimatum had the desired effect: scared the bejeebers out of them and kept them out of serious trouble.

I had made my weekly pilgrimage to see my car, and I was in my own world. He startled me out of my daze when he spied me outside drooling on the dealership showroom window. "Hey kid. What 'cha doing out here hanging around?"

Embarrassed, I started to get on my bike and make a run for it, but he was so cute I instinctively turned toward him. "I like that T-Bird. It's cool."

"Well, get your Daddy to buy it for you."

What a smart aleck. Everything I'd heard about him was true. Big head and big mouth.

"He would, but I can't drive yet." I didn't say what I thought. Not all of us have a Daddy that buys us everything we want. Some of us are taught to work for what we get. Too foreign a concept I was sure for Eddie Ray Simone.

"How old are you twerp?"

"My name is Claire, and I'm not a twerp. It's none of your business how old I am. I have to go now."

"You better quit coming around here, or I'll tell my dad. This is a place of business."

"Yeah? Then what are you doing here?"

"Hey, short stuff, my dad owns this dealership, and I help him run the place. We even have a race car that I'm going to drive someday."

"Well, goody for you." I yelled back at him as I pedaled away.

The idea! That jerk thought he could tell me what to do and where I could go. He didn't know who he was dealing with. Why did he have to be so good-looking? His good looks stuck in my pea brain. His blond hair was styled perfectly in a crew cut with sides smoothed back in a ducktail finished off with sky blue eyes that shone right through you. He wore his collar turned up. On most guys, that looked stupid but not on Eddie Ray. I returned to the dealership the next week right on schedule. The T-bird was there to greet me, and so was Eddie Ray.

"Hey, I told you not to come back. What do you want and why are you here?"

"I came to see my turquoise Thunderbird."

"It's not turquoise. It's peacock blue. And it's not your Thunderbird. What makes you think you can afford this car? It's way expensive and way too cool for you."

I wouldn't admit defeat and ignored his insults. "My dad will probably get that car for me and keep it until I'm old enough. He's a lawyer and can afford it. He's John Chastain."

"Big deal. Did you bring a check?"

He thought he was so funny. Why am I talking to this fool? He's such a swelled head and not nice—a total waste of my time.

"Don't you know who I am? I'm Eddie Ray Simone, and I work here. I might possibly get you a good deal on this car." Hard to believe but his smirk was bigger than his ego.

I decided to give up trying to make this meeting go anywhere. I didn't realize until now what a good thing our paths hadn't crossed before.

"You're not a nice person. Someday you might be sorry you were so rude. Why don't you grow up? Nobody cares about your tiny dealership in this tiny town."

I was stunned by my own outburst. He made a strange waving motion. No telling what that meant.

"Let's call a truce, okay. Nothin' personal. It's just that we can't allow a bunch of rug rats to hang out around here. Might get hurt or somethin'. It's bad for business."

That was the beginning of my friendship with Eddie Ray Simone. I would see him at the Dairy Mart with his buddies, and he would say a quick "Hello Twerp." I saw him at the movies with his date and nearly choked on my popcorn when he said hi. I asked my dad about the Simones and told him I had met Eddie Ray. He told me they were nice people and that Mr. Simone had bought a 1956 Ford to drag race and that he would like to go see them race if I wanted to go. We went to as many races as possible, and our family and the Simones established a friendship. I knew more about Eddie Ray than just about anyone. Sometime early on, I began to see him differently, and a massive crush started to replace my annoyance. In spite of our rocky start, we became friends. He liked my boldness and admired my standing up for myself. But then he also called me Goody Two Shoes. At least, we recognized where we stood with each other. He thought of me as his little sister and, like it or not, I would forever be Twerp.

At the age of fifteen on Saturdays, he switched from merely hanging around to doing real work in the dealership. The rules were clear—no messing around. Eddie Ray had a defined list of chores. Clean the tools, clean the machinery, clean the floor, clean the toilets. The obvious goal: keep Eddie busy. He was not to run out of work. When the race car appeared, his outlook on cars took a 360-degree turn. His dad asked Nick, eight years older than Eddie Ray, to drive the race car. Nick was at the dealership 24/7 with Eddie Ray as his constant shadow.

His parents went to the bigger races mainly to show the Chevy folks that their Ford was a real contender. The Ford could outrun them. During the Texas Championships, Eddie Ray took it upon himself to run around the racetrack and the bleachers spreading the news that their Ford could and undoubtedly would beat any Chevy. Mostly, people just grinned and nodded saying to each other, "Isn't he cute?" No one seemed particularly impressed or curious. That is, until after the race was over. They had won the Texas Championships and were on their way to the U.S. Nationals in Great Bend, Kansas. Eddie Ray was a big fish in small waters, but he had his eye on bigger.

Nick took Eddie Ray in tow which proved to be almost as time-consuming as the car. Nick would ask for a screwdriver and get a wrench. Ask for a wrench, and he'd get a ratchet. Eddie Ray just kept asking a million questions, dumb as a rock in the beginning but determined to learn. When they worked on the car after hours, Eddie stayed into the night until his mother dragged him out. That was the beginning of Eddie Ray's fascination with cars and racing. As if a shortage of girls was a problem, racing attracted females like a fire sale at Macy's.

The Simones' 1957 Ford drag car was the first super stock car in the area that ever broke 100 mph—good enough to win the Texas Regionals and the US Nationals. Eddie Ray surprised everyone (including himself), and he actually began to understand the inner workings of a car. The next year he would get his driver's license. He was on the hunt for the perfect car to drag race, but his parents had other plans—not so fast Eddie Ray.

Eddie Ray broke the news that his dad had to be in Mexico City on another business venture over the summer, so Eddie Ray's next three months were already planned. It was hard to believe. He would spend the summer with his parents in Mexico City. Were there no limits to this guy's coolness? It wasn't hard to figure out that his parents were doing their best to distract him so he would have to put his drag racing on hold.

Mexico City offered many attractions. Drag racing was not one of them, but road racing was. His dad's business partner Paul Quinton had mentioned that he wanted to take everyone to a road race. Eddie Ray could not have planned the next two months any better. Quinton taught Eddie all the basics—cornering, braking, shifting, how to hit an early or late apex, how to maneuver around a road course–all expertly demonstrated in his mother's 1957 Ford retractable hardtop. "I have to go over the mountain to Cuernavaca on business. Would you like to take a ride?" Quinton grinned. That was the magic phrase. The old man was as smooth behind the wheel as a professional. But it got even better. He introduced Eddie Ray to his nephew Brian who ran with a bunch of guys whose parents all worked in Mexico City. A bunch of ex-pat brats who ran in a pack which was completely unknown to Eddie. It was well known that it was best not to venture out on your own here. Quinton assured them that the Larks was not a gang. It was a club. To small-town Eddie, this was a unique concept—you need group support to watch your backside. The mission of the Larks was simple: have more fun than anyone should, always stick together and watch out for each other's backs and did someone say "girls," well, even better! Eddie Ray was in. Since Brian's dad was a high-ranking official in the government in Mexico City, all Brian had to do was flash his I.D. They were ushered in anywhere they wanted to go. It was an easy adjustment to be men about town at sixteen.

One Saturday night they headed to the nicest restaurant in town, Fernando's. As soon as they arrived, Eddie Ray was ready to leave. He did not stand in long lines. "Oh, let's go. Just look at this mess. We'll never get in." He pointed to the line that wrapped around the building and down the street.

Brian seemed amused. "Oh yeah, put your money where your mouth is. I'll bet you $10 we do get in, no prob. "

Brian flashed his driver's license and in they went ahead of everyone including Eddie Ray's parents. Needless to say, they had their choice of female companionship for the evening. Even though his drag racing was on hold, he had the most memorable summer of his life and would always remember the Larks. His introduction into the benefits of racing and being the center of attention just made him want more.

We were pretty much Eddie's groupies of our day—lowest echelon of course. His adventures and dreams were big and legendary. When Eddie Ray returned to town, we resumed where we had left off. We started hanging around the same kids at the Dairy Mart and packed ourselves in someone's old car to go watch him race. The Mexico City adventure opened a new world. He had his driver's license and a part-time job and was able to afford his own car—a 1958 Ford two-door post, stick shift, V-8.

It was no secret he street raced, but that was a big no-no and totally off-limits for me. As much as I wanted to be in the in-crowd, I was generally not a rule breaker, and there were some risks I would not take. He continued to spend most of his high school years street racing and winning at the local tracks and nearby national drag strips. But he still had the stigma of racing a Ford against the hot Chevys and losing. One night after a race, we all went to the local drive-in as was our usual routine. We hung out and hung on his every word as he explained his latest escapades and plans for his racing career.

My dad was picking up burgers to take home for his and Mother's supper and stopped by the group to say hi. He put his hand on Eddie Ray's shoulder and grinned. "Eddie Ray, looks like you can draw and keep a crowd. Have you considered a career in politics?" Later at home, Dad commented that it looked as if Eddie was "holding court" and was amazed at how our crowd was so intent on Eddie's every word. I guess basically it boiled down to Eddie Ray's magnetism plus we had nothing better to do that offered this level of fantasy. We were watching history in the making. This guy from our nowhere town had us convinced that he was going to be somebody and that was enough for us.

A shot of reality hit me between the eyes at my first and last sprint car race. I spent one Saturday night watching him race on a dirt track getting bombarded head-to-toe by tiny mud balls while he spun around the dirt track in a sprint car. The small unstable car with the wing on top looked like a ridiculous toy to me, but Eddie Ray couldn't get enough. It was hot and noisy, and I came away smelling like the inside of an exhaust pipe and looking like a giant mud ball. How would it ever be any different? I looked squarely into the face of the future. Somehow I couldn't visualize me a permanent fixture in this scenario. I was a perfectionist with my own ideas and goals and wouldn't change. I was too prissy and too uptight for racing and too controlling for someone like Eddie Ray.

We never knew what to expect from Eddie Ray except for one chronic condition. He suffered from constant car dilemma. He needed a driver but also a car for road racing. His solution was simple. He needed a Corvette! It would be perfect for road racing and would be a cool driver. But there was a catch: there was no way he could afford it.

Eddie Ray turned to me. "Maybe I can get my parents to buy me a car." He had luck on his side. He was an only child whose parents made a habit of doting. He counted on his parents to come up with a plan, and they did not disappoint. He was not above being bribed, so they insisted he go to college. In return, they would help him buy the car he had to have which was a used 1957 Arctic Blue Corvette.

He was still working at the dealership and joined a Corvette club that had his same vision—racing and partying. The club was affiliated with the Sports Car Club of America, so Eddie Ray decided it was a good way to get into local road racing. One of his first outings was a Sports Car Club of America sanctioned event on a Sunday after a weekend of drag racing. Another member who had been racing for years offered to give him some pointers.

After Eddie Ray's first run, Tom had quite a bit to say. "Erratic and jerky but you show promise," he grinned. "We'll practice keeping control through the corners instead of letting the car slide. Smooth into the corner and into the straightaway—that's it. Sounds easy I know but it takes practice. Kind of like handling a woman, you know. Gotta be so smooth she never knows what's happenin'." Tom seemed like a guy who spoke from experience, so Eddie Ray paid attention. "The car must be an extension of you, ol' man."

The beginning of Eddie Ray's road racing showed he had the beginner's touch—so anxious to drive the course as fast as possible he was fighting the car, hitting the gas too hard, spinning the rear tires. He had the racer instincts, but lacked control and had to learn to find the apex and when and how to brake in turns. He had to learn patience to keep the car in control and learn the finesse of acceleration and the trained eye to know where the car should be on the racetrack and the overall handling of the car. Eddie Ray had the confidence and razor-sharp focus of a successful racer. There was no space and no place for mental clutter in the helmet until after the checkered flag.

He was still hooked on the rawness of street racing and the drags, but he was ready to upgrade to his first love of road racing. The 1957 Vette came with strings, and his parents didn't hesitate or waver. They wanted him to have an education. He would attend college in exchange for their helping him buy the car.

"Twerp, I'm going to try this college thing, so I won't be around much. You know, this is an offer I can't turn down. I'll take a few college courses, race on the weekends with a much better car and have fun. Perfect plan, huh?"

"Sure, Eddie. Who are you kidding? We both know college isn't for you."

"Right, right. You miss the point. It'll be the way to get my Vette. I have a plan. Besides, don't you want to be the first to go for a ride with me?" He gave me his Hollywood grin. He was part salesman and part con artist. It was difficult to tell the difference.

"You know, Twerp, you're goin' to have to hurry up and grow up. I can't wait forever on you. Maybe we can get together after I make the big time. Then it'll be our time, what's say?"

I smiled. "Right, Eddie. I'll be sure and hold my breath. I know how you love blue."

The next thing I knew, I was riding in the passenger seat of his 1957 Arctic Blue Corvette. "How'd you like to be my navigator on a road rally?"

"Sure, I guess. What do I have to do?" It sounded fun and not too difficult; just seemed to be a matter of teamwork. How hard could it be?

The next Saturday, we joined fourteen other Corvette Club members for a rally in time & distance in the country with our final destination Pop's Drive-In, 50 miles away with a one-hour time limit. I had been given a crash (poor choice of words) course in my role as navigator. I was given my tools: a map showing the route (with no deviations allowed), a stopwatch, calculator and pencil and paper to keep up with his speed and distance. There were three checkpoints along the route. Each car got in line to begin the race and advanced to the start position. The starter then handed the navigator a time slip showing their exact starting time and then yelled, "Go!". The time allotted to finish was set at exactly 60 minutes, not a second less or more. Eddie Ray started aggressively and yelled "doing 45" and then "50 now" which caught me totally off-guard and I did not hit the stopwatch.

He snapped, "Claire, you've got to keep up." This would be a long afternoon. He called me by my actual name—a bad sign.

He would mentally calculate how fast he needed to go for what distance to meet the average of 50 mph. I was to hit the stopwatch when he yelled out his speed that varied from the specified average mph. Then I would calculate how fast and how far he would need to drive to meet the average. I was in panic mode. At the first checkpoint, the worker recorded our car number as we went by.

The checkpoint was 15 miles, and I stated the time was 14.50. "No and no! That's not right! It's closer to 12.5," yelled an annoyed Eddie Ray. "Use your brain, Claire. We go .8333 in a minute, and we've gone 15 miles, what do you think?? Basic math??"

I was furious and near tears. How dare him! He had his nerve talking down to me. He's nothing but a glorified grease monkey! "Whatever you say, Mr. Bigshot Know-It-All. Just drive and calculate yourself, you're a Magic One Man Band—the Fast Eddie Ray can do it all!!" The silence from both sides of the car was deafening for the remaining thirty-five miles. I should have known this was risky business. Get in the way of Eddie Ray's winning and suffer the consequences. I stood my ground and stayed annoyed, but the burgers and milkshakes were great. My needs were simple, and I had a huge mental block grasping the earth-shattering significance of it all.

Change was in the air. Eddie Ray had flunked out of college and had gone serious about racing. Libby was the first to tell me. She had seen him at Patsy's, a favorite hangout in the neighboring town, with the same blond draped all over him. There was rumor of driving school and going professional.

I'd been around Eddie and the pits long enough to know the drill. Racing meant girls and beer flowing and party, party, party. We were outgrowing each other. I had no desire to be one of his party girls even if I had been old enough, but plenty of others were in line. I could hardly wait to meet the new flavor of the month. Sunday races should be interesting.

I went by the pit area to say hey to Eddie and got an eyeful. I spotted a good-looking blonde leaning over his car with her 36Ds falling out over the 283 and her gushing over Eddie Ray. He and his buddies were busy doing their own gushing.

"Hey Twerp. Want 'cha to meet Vicki. She likes to race and is thinking of getting her own Vette."

The blonde looked up at him and smiled and smugly pressed against him.

I made an effort to be interested, but Eddie was moving on, and so was I. He was going to driving school, blah, blah, blah. I was out of my league. It was time to back away. Somehow my good sense kicked in, and I yielded to the caution signs of trouble ahead. Fun while it lasted but over now. He would forever be Fast Eddie Ray, and I simply wouldn't be able to keep up.

The last I heard he was road racing at Lime Rock Race Park in Lakeville, Connecticut which was his dream and eventually he got the necessary big money sponsors. It all sounded the same to me, but I knew the difference. He had entered the intense, stress-filled world of large-scale, big business, and giant stakes. Once you are bitten by the racing bug, you are addicted. But isn't that true of most anything you feel passionately about? Eddie had the desire and intensity to be a great race car driver, but Twerp would not be along for the ride. I was done. I'd hardly noticed a couple of years had gone by since some city slicker came to town to get a good deal and drove my dream car away. Fast Eddie Ray Simone. 1956 Thunderbird. *Way cooler than me.*

Chapter 16. Summer of 1959

This was a summer to be remembered. It began as routinely as any other with no hint of something big on the horizon. I had my dark secret hope that I shared with my closest friends. I would learn to water ski but in the most glamorous way. His family had the fastest, shiniest, most expensive boat on the lake. This would be the summer that certain cute boy would ask me to join his elite group on his Chris Craft. It was the most exhilarating, all-encompassing thought in my tiny brain. I did have one overwhelming concern that filled me with growing apprehension. I still had not yet developed to fill the top half of my two-piece. I had the dubious distinction of being known as the flat-chested brainy one. My girlfriends were oh so helpful. Giggling hysterically, "Claire, here use this scarf" or "Claire, try a wad of toilet paper" or Kleenex or any other various stuffings that were handy. I was assured any of these could solve my problem with one caution: make sure the padding doesn't escape to float on its own. Thanks a lot. I was not convinced and mildly amused by their recommendations. I was convinced that I could fake it. Besides, there were other ways that did not require me to show my lack of endowment.

Thursday night was the most happening night of the week for me, but not so for the chaperones, closer to a recurring nightmare. The gym had been outfitted with railings and soft barricades to cushion our falls so that we could roller skate. Jam-packed with kids of every age, relentless noise and my favorite—the *music*—the makeshift "skating rink" was the place to be. It was a confined, ear-piercing din of roller skates, thuds and crashes, and rock and roll booming at ear-splitting decibels from hopelessly old, scratchy speakers. Kids were crying and screaming; skirmishes broke out as bullies tried to take over the floor; and the constant grinding of metal rollers hitting the wood floor blasted through all the other deafening noises.

Laced uptight and snow white, it was the virgin outing for my Chicago roller skates. I was fixated on the problem now facing me of how to keep them in their pristine condition. Somehow these skates elevated me from the other, younger skaters and their ugly strapped-on-primitive skates. I was not hugely concerned that I did not know how to skate. How hard could it be? Besides, I looked like a skater. I secretly suspected that my favorite turquoise full, circular skirt and coordinated peasant blouse accompanied by such professional skates made up for my lack of skating ability. Another dream of mine (at least for this year) was about to come true. I was going to be a skater!

I was increasingly aware of my parents' watchful eyes and the inevitable. I must get my back off the wall and let go of the railing to enter the counterclockwise flow of chaos. My parents expected some great things from me. In no uncertain terms, they assured me repeatedly that these specifically-requested and specially-ordered skates from Chicago were too expensive. It better be worth the hard-earned money spent. I had invested all my savings for these skates, and now I was completely broke. So terrified and shaky, away I went, skates zooming ahead to make my dashing debut that gave bystanders more than they bargained for. I landed hard on my backside, feet flying out and up, throwing my big circular skirt and petticoats over my head. It was my vivid hot pink Fruit of the Looms that flashed like neon to every skater, parent and innocent bystander. In spite of Mother's repeated warnings, I would have it no other way and as she predicted, wearing all those petticoats proved to be my undoing. At that moment, the vision of my being a graceful, effortless skater floating on the floor distorted into a Three Stooges comedy sideshow. But I refused to leave the floor. It was the first of what seemed like a hundred rear-end landings. My new goal was to skate one round without falling backward. After two bruising, exhausting hours, the long-awaited announcement came, "all skaters off the floor." My classmates made sure the embarrassment of my debut as a roller skater stayed with me for the duration of my school years. I would not live long enough to live it down. I should cross roller derby queen off my list.

In summer, the local ball field was converted from football to baseball. I loved to play baseball but, on these occasions, it was a spectator sport. Farm teams would periodically play exhibition games which pumped some much-needed life in our small town. My dad sold peanuts and popcorn for the local boys and girls club. As the daughter of a civic-minded, small-town businessman, I was expected to make an appearance at the games a few times each summer. It was my job to lug big cloth sacks of goodies while Dad assumed the role of carnival barker, repeatedly yelling "Get your hot (not really) peanuts and fresh (rarely) popcorn." He made sure every kid at the game had a snack free. I, too, was well cared for. I ate most of what I carried. My dad would shake his head disapprovingly and send me repeatedly to the truck for replenished supplies. At the end of the night, he was pulling dollars out of his wallet to pay for all the goodies I ate (fee for my "help") and for all the freebies he had given away.

Summer of '59 was memorable for another event for Libby and me. Okay, it was more comical than momentous. We had noticed the boys, and a few had noticed us, but not the ones we were interested in. Mother mentioned that the Methodist preacher's son was a nice boy who apparently had her approval.

"Claire, Joel is such a good-looking young man, why don't you two go to a movie?"

"Oh, Mother, I don't know. He is always on that scooter of his. He's kind of goofy."

"Well, then, how about the Baptist preacher's son? He seems presentable."

I mentioned it to Libby. Immediately I noticed the familiar evil glint.

Her blue eyes danced with devilment. "Yeah, that would be great. We should double date."

I was curious. "Okay. Who exactly is going on this 'double date'?"

"Well, you and I will double date Joel."

She threw back her head laughing like a hyena.

"Very funny. Okay, you go with the Baptist preacher's son. Isn't his name Clayton? How about that, Miss Comedian."

"Okay. I will ask him, so there. You ask Joel. Our first date—how perfect."

In two weeks, one quiet Sunday afternoon, we were in the movie theater on our first date—double date—together. There were five of us—the two preachers' sons, Libby and I, and the red scooter. Joel rode his scooter to the theater and spent most of the afternoon making countless trips outside to make sure it was still there. We went for ice cream afterward, but the best part of the date was when it was over. We couldn't quit laughing.

"Claire, don't worry, Joel is too busy petting his scooter. You won't have to fight him off." Libby wouldn't let go of it.

She was in top form. That was a date we did not want to forget; it stood the test of time and stayed funny. It did break up the monotony of the summer and the continuing saga of a glamorous mystery girl coming to town.

Chapter 17. Stranger in Town

Her glowing reviews hit town like a lightning bolt. Between my dad with his noteworthy tidbits and the juicy bits from the street, I heard enough gossip to go around for all of us. But I had yet to experience our ability to make a person a celebrity before she even got to town.

Word of mouth at supersonic speed is the small town equivalent of "hot off the press." We've been known to spread news before it happens or even if it *never* happens. Speedy communication via the grapevine works. But rarely was there any news worth repeating. So for now, we were unaware. School was out, and the town was ours. Living out on the Ranch, Libby was insulated and missed most of the town rumor mill, but I was privy to everything that was going on and anything that was rumored to go on.

I first heard the rumor from my mother of all people. She did not repeat gossip. She and my dad had spent a lifetime building a small business here. Reputation and image were practically sacred. For some reason, she decided to share her nugget of information. While she was in the beauty shop that afternoon, Delores said that her niece from California was coming to live with her. I tripped getting to the phone to call Libby. We couldn't phone our fabulous four fast enough for a last-minute sleepover. This was big, and we needed to pool our information to figure out what was going on and be the first to know.

These four were no strangers to hearsay. We were literally abuzz with the news, all talking at once, and trying desperately to be the first to break the story and be the one who knew the most. A new girl was coming to our town. That in itself was news enough. Rarely did we see a new face, and it was even rarer for someone to move here. Not many people came here to stay voluntarily. It was not a bad place. There were no jobs. If you didn't own land or a business, you drove 60 or 70 miles to work in the city. Most families lived here for generations, and it was just a matter of well, heritage or maybe bondage, depending on your viewpoint. Every now and then a kid or someone's cousin from the city would visit a relative for the summer to enjoy the country because it was a novelty. Libby was an exception—she was one of the few who became one of us. Sherilyn, who took great pride in her ability to be the first to know and broadcast it all, described the new girl as practically a movie star who lived in California. Not possible, we said in unison. She wouldn't be coming here if that were true. We looked at each other. Or would she?

Undaunted, Sherilyn the know-it-all continued, "Well, she has performed at the Hollywood Playhouse, and her father is a bigwig movie producer."

"She is coming here to live with her aunt," I proudly contributed my tidbit.

"Yeah, because she lives with her dad in Hollywood, and he is being sent to a faraway place on a movie assignment," said Laurie as she continued her blow-by-blow report. "She's a junior and seventeen. Someone said she is going to be an actress and can sing and dance."

I was skeptical. I would wait and see. I was calm on the outside, but my stomach was churning. For the first time in a long time, the air was charged with electricity awakening the sleepy town. The idea of it was intoxicating: someone from Hollywood here.

By the first of August, I wanted summer to be over. I was ready for school to start. My curiosity had taken over, and I was bored waiting for it. I wanted to see that new girl. Then one-blast-from-the-furnace August afternoon, the day came. Libby called me from Emmett's Texaco jabbering and so obviously flabbergasted, I barely understood her.

"She's here, she's here!! She and her dad just drive through town in a white convertible with the top down. She has dark red hair."

I didn't get the significance of her hair color, but I guess that was all she saw of the girl, her head. The convertible was certainly significant, and actually, I was focused on the car. Thinking back, I recall asking what kind of car. That was not the thing to say. My friend was out of control and out of patience.

"What? You want to know about the car? That's just crazy! What's wrong with you?" Well, we rarely saw convertibles either. As you can tell, I was having trouble with the concept of a budding starlet coming to town.

I would not give in to all this brouhaha and would reserve judgment. I did not customarily hero-worship. In fact, I was pretty much against it. The exception was my dad whom I adored and maybe John Wayne. But let her come, I will decide for myself.

That opportunity came sooner than I expected at the next Friday night baseball game. Dad and I were peddling the heck out of those peanuts and popcorn and in she walked. Our small plot of civilization stood still. Everyone in the bleachers turned her way. We had known for weeks she was coming. Although we did not know what to expect, we suspected it would be great. She was tall, slim, and graceful when she walked like gliding on air. Her shiny, reddish brown hair hung down her back in a glorious, long ponytail which was longer than any human ponytail I had ever seen. She had a quality we were not accustomed to in Podunk, Texas.

People started running over to her. "Oh, good grief, what a mob scene." I jolted myself back to reality. I was glad for once to be busy helping my dad. I did notice that she stayed long enough to make an appearance and to make certain everyone saw her. Typical, I scowled.

Chapter 18. Joanna

I took off my heavy bag of snacks and loaded the truck. All I heard was a buzzing noise. People had gone berserk. Oh, you missed seeing her up close, said one. Her name is Joanna Reyes. She is so pretty, and she is so friendly and nice. She seems like she knows us. She's not a stranger at all. Not likely I thought. Show me a pretty girl and I'll show you stuck-up and stuck on herself. At fourteen, with raging acne and tomboy tendencies, plus an added dose of awkward, I felt that stuck-up pretty much described all attractive females. I was proud that I did manage with sufficient effort to keep my thoughts to myself. Sour grapes and all.

The first day of school and the halls were chaotic even in our small school. This was my first year of high school, and I was already traumatized. I was also annoyed. Why did we have to add to this mix of craziness the arrival of this new girl Joanna? Oh, well, I said to myself, get used to it. You will be face-to-face during cheerleader tryouts at the end of the week. Even though I was a freshman, there was no doubt I would be a cheerleader. It was practically my birthright. She was the outsider and should earn her spot and learn her place. Ah, I was such a naïve, young thing.

I had practiced my routine at least 100 times. Even my snooty friends begrudgingly said I was good enough to win, although I would be competing against experienced cheerleaders from last year. That morning, I managed to find the iron and pressed my shorts and blouse to crisp perfection. My PF Flyers were bright white and brand new. I had generously applied the orangey, smelly self-tanner. I was ready.

She was the center of attention. Our girls' basketball coach, who was also our cheer coach, presented her to the group. What is she, royalty, I silently pouted. Well, she was pretty. She had that hair. Still deep reddish brown, shiny and wavy, and still in that incredibly long ponytail. I could not take my eyes off her skin, olive brown and beyond clear. Not only was there not one blemish, there was also not one pore. But most startling was her smile. Once the introduction was made, she acknowledged us with a slight wave. Of course, nothing got past me. There were certain physical qualities I noticed in everyone and in a certain order. But in her case, I noticed something unique about her hands. Her fingers were long and slender (not unusual), but her fingertips slightly curled up. I had never seen hands like that. Then she said a few words and smiled making sure she was looking just at you and drawing you in. That smile was dazzling. Her teeth were perfect and chalk white—not a toothy grin but not all gum either. I was totally out of patience with myself. "What is this," I muttered, trying to analyze what was happening here. She is not what I call gorgeous but mesmerizing. At that moment I wanted to be like her. Her eyes were deer-like and deep brown with tinges of hazel. But the most striking of all was the kindness within her eyes. She exuded all the qualities I wanted but lacked. Open. Confident. Inspired. I was in a Joanna trance.

She was a fabulous cheerleader who evidently had come out of the womb tumbling and had spent her life in gymnastics. Surprise. I had not. I might manage a cartwheel on a good day, and shaking my pompoms was an effort. It would have to be next year for me; not much of a consolation. When I timidly went over to congratulate her and introduce myself, she instantly calmed my nervousness. She hugged me and called me "sweetie." Surprisingly, I didn't want to slug her or even take offense. Somehow coming from her the term lost its sting and didn't seem the least bit patronizing. She complimented my cheerleading and offered to help me. I appreciated her trying to make me feel better, but I was terribly disappointed. I would miss the highlight of the year and the most exciting part of being a cheerleader—going to the city to attend the well-known cheerleading academy led by Rudy "Rah Rah" Rutherford. She asked what sports I played, and I assured her I played every sport they would let me—basketball, volleyball and baseball and even ran some track. She said, "Great. We will be friends because I love to play sports, too." My mind was whirling.

She could be the big sister I longed for but never had. In the span of one day, Joanna transformed from suspicious outsider to my goddess big sis. I suspected she had taken a liking to me for some mysterious reason. Maybe I was her good deed for the year. Anyway, she saw something in me that sparked her interest—call it potential for lack of a better term. I cautioned myself to keep a lid on my Joanna awe…she didn't strike me as someone who liked being fawned over…just being the center of attention would suffice.

The next weeks and months proved to be the most invigorating of my young life. I was playing basketball on the high school B team. After practice, Joanna gave me one-on-one pointers. Our hard work paid off. I progressed from being able to walk and carry the basketball to a dribbling fool! I learned how to outmaneuver guards who were bigger, taller and slower than I. What I lacked in stature, I made up in sheer grit. I became a scrappy rebounder, and a dependable shot maker. Handling the basketball became second nature to me. I soon was substituting for the starting forwards playing an increasing part of each game. The coach even commented that, if I continued to improve, I could be a starter my sophomore year.

Joanna took the town by storm with her ingenuity. She was fearless which totally captivated me, the little mouse, scared of my own shadow. Sometimes her ideas generated just pure fun. At the first football game, she arrived an hour early and stood at the gate with pompoms in hand welcoming every person who arrived. No cheerleader had ever done this. She and my dad saw that everyone (whether old, infirm or otherwise) who needed a folding chair got one, set up and ready. She persuaded the cheer coach that the cheerleaders needed "little sisters." So at each game, a different pint-sized version of a cheerleader was leading a cheer or two or just hanging out with the big girls.

There were a few problems: not so much from the townspeople but from, shall we say, authority? If she had an idea, she would generally just go with it. Well, even in "eye-blink, you miss it," Texas, that policy does not work. "She has to be corralled," the principal said. My dad was on the school board and reluctantly took on the task, although there was an obvious conflict of interest. She and my dad were frequently in cahoots about changes that needed to be made in the town. She came for dinner often and loved sitting around our big Formica table in the kitchen laughing and talking. She was part of our family. Dad would wink at her and laugh, and I noticed his eyes twinkled more. I was glad to have her as a member of the family, but I worried that he showed too much interest in Joanna mainly because I saw Mother watching both of them closely. She seemed to be irritated at Dad, and I noticed her giving him a glare which was unusual. Something was bothering her, and I did not understand what because she liked Joanna. I shrugged it off because Joanna and my dad were alike in so many ways. They were both civic-minded and never content with the status quo. Their mantra was change always to be considered as an improvement.

One evening after Joanna left and I had gone to bed, I heard Mother and Dad having a lively discussion about Joanna. Mother said something about being careful that people don't get the wrong idea about Joanna. Dad said that was ridiculous she is like a daughter to me, but Mother insisted, "You know how people like to talk. We don't want anyone to get hurt by gossip especially Joanna."

Joanna continued to come up with new tasks for me to accomplish. The way she put it, "Claire, the sky's the limit for you. I want you to be the best and to be everything I know you can be." She mentioned that she wanted to teach me Spanish.

"Claire, I'd love to teach you and Libby some of the basics if you want to learn. Maybe we could find a few hours a couple days a week—just conversational stuff."

Oh, Joanna. You've done it now. I looked at my mother's beaming face which was practically lighting up the room.

"Joanna, that is so nice of you. We'll just have to figure out when we can work it in. Let's see if we can do it after football and basketball season." I was making an effort to be nice and trying to think of one good reason to learn to speak Spanish. Well, let's see, Joanna was bilingual. I barely spoke English. Maybe some conversational Spanish was a good idea. I reminded myself of my habitual hastiness. I needed to be on guard because of my lack of foresight and another *lost opportunity.*

The most shocking change came the night before a game when she convinced the other cheerleaders that the uniforms were old-fashioned. They all promptly shortened their cheerleading skirts from slightly above the knee to mid-thigh. You talk about causing mass hysteria; the administration went into a tailspin. The school board was called into emergency session, and Joanna was called onto the carpet. She was suspended for one game, and she vowed from then on to follow the rules. After that fiasco, she consulted my dad before implementing her ideas.

She also brought much-needed change and improvement to our town. One afternoon when she stopped to give an older lady a ride who was struggling to carry groceries home, she encouraged the three grocery stores to rotate delivering groceries to the old and sick who weren't able to get to town. One grocer hired some of the older boys to deliver groceries. She convinced my dad and the Lions Club to set up a Christmas tree in town for the first time in decades. On Christmas Eve, everyone gathered at the tree to celebrate and sing carols. Such a simple act of coming together at Christmas brought the entire community closer, and it was another opportunity to be with friends and neighbors. She organized a small chorus that sang at the hospital and nursing home during the holidays. She was acutely aware of her surroundings and the needs of people in our town.

She organized some of the junior and senior girls to be candy stripers at the local hospital and nursing home alternating for a few hours each week. Previously most of the volunteers came from the local women's clubs. She was instrumental in our becoming aware of what was going on in our town and who needed what. Ignorance was not an excuse. She was recognized by the local Chamber of Commerce for her community involvement and was asked to speak at the Toastmasters Club banquet. Mr. Kipperson at the hometown newspaper referred to her as a motivational speaker beyond her years.

Joanna still had the time and energy to be one-half of the school dream couple. She started dating the catch of the town almost from the day she arrived here. Johnny Mack played football and basketball and was the smartest person in high school. No one had any doubt he would go on to bigger and better. He and Joanna couldn't have been more perfectly matched. They were seniors and had already planned to marry someday, but were determined to finish high school and go to college together. He had been accepted at the university where he would study engineering and play football.

It was one of those perfect Friday fall evenings in early November under the lights. The weather was cool and clear and the excitement of the Thanksgiving holidays was in the air. The crowd was enthusiastic about the promise of things to come like beating the pants off this visiting team and sending them home with their tails between their legs. As the pre-game warm-up dragged on, I decided to take advantage of the lull and ran to the restroom. As I turned the corner of the ladies room, I heard the most horrible sound of my young life. The crowd gasped, and a hush fell over the small stadium. There had to be trouble. I looked on the field and saw #18 lying on the ground. Johnny Mack had run out and caught a pass, thrown the ball back and then got back in line and collapsed. The field was chaotic with activity and then nothing. Our players were in a circle. Some were sobbing, and some were sitting on the field with their heads in their hands. We were all in shock. The coach looked helpless and dazed as several players and my dad put Johnny Mack on a stretcher and drove away in the ambulance. He could not be revived and was pronounced dead from *cardiac arrest.*

We were overwhelmed with sorrow and disbelief. We had lost one of our own. He was eighteen years old and had not even begun his adult life. We felt cheated, angry and confused. We tried to console his family and Joanna, but our words seemed vacant and meaningless. She did not leave his family's side for days. Just having her near comforted them and made them feel closer to their son. Although she was devastated, her focus was on the others who needed her strength. She tried her best to hide her sorrow. Her underlying grief proved to be an unrelenting monster that demanded her full and undivided attention and would not be denied. In a delayed reaction to her grief, she became almost dysfunctional. For the first three months after his death, I was worried that she would not recover from the shock, sorrow and heartache of her loss.

Joanna refused to give in to the bitterness. She regained her resolve, and a new maturity and strength took the place of the devastating sadness. In her desire to recover, this tragedy allowed her to show her weakness. She showed that she needed our support. We learned about her and her background and the inner Joanna who had previously been off-limits. She leaned on my dad after Johnny Mack's death and told me she could not have made it through this tough time without him.

"Claire, you know how much I admire your dad. He and I have become so close in the last few months. He has been such a big help and a strong shoulder to lean on. You are so lucky to have him."

I loved Joanna and was glad to have her as part of the family, and her relationship with my dad was innocent. But Mother was concerned about what people saw and thought. She knew how little it takes to cause talk when there is a pretty girl, so she was concerned about Joanna as well. For sure, it was probably a good thing that she was leaving for college and to follow her dreams. She had her heart set on New York to be an actress and to be on Broadway. No one and nothing would stand in her way.

She stayed with us for two years. I dare say that each one of us was affected in some way by Joanna. She brought out the best in us and our town. She cried and laughed with us, taught us and learned from us, became one of us. The person she was unfolded before us and became more than her beautiful physical presence. Her mother died when Joanna was born, and her father did not remarry. She longed to belong, and California did not fill that void. She showed an overwhelming desire to be accepted in our town. Now we understood why. She embraced us all—old, young, sick, well-to-do or not. She inspired us to do and to be more than we thought possible. I never saw her treat any person badly. She had her faults for sure. She was so enthusiastic and focused that she failed to analyze the consequences. She was overbearing, intense and driven to get things done: a pony-tailed dynamo. She dominated the conversation, the meeting, the game, the dance—she demanded her rightful place as the center of attention. On the serious side, she was obsessive about her responsibility. Her mother died giving her life. She once told me, "I owe it to her to use all I have in the time I have to do the most I can."

The day inevitably came when she graduated, and she had to leave us. She had tried out for the University Lone Star Strutters and had received her acceptance letter from Director Cora Mae Jarvis. That was no small accomplishment. Cora Mae's strict requirements were legendary, competition was fierce, and the coveted invitation to join the prestigious high-kickers reserved for a precious few. As she climbed into the car, she hugged me and whispered, "Adios angelito and May God Bless. I am going to miss you so much. This town will always have a special place deep in my heart." It was the summer of 1961 as we said good-bye and Joanna drove away.

She was gone. We consoled each other and laughed that, with Joanna going to university, Cora Mae could be in danger of losing her job. We had to settle back into the routine of life as before—before Joanna. I hardly remembered life in our town before she arrived. I smiled. At last, my tunnel vision beautiful girl theory was shot to smithereens! Joanna was one beautiful, talented gal just as beautiful on the inside. Amazing. I accepted she was human, but she was also extraordinary.

When she left us, for sure, she left a void, and she left making us better. The contributions she continually made to our town and our lives would make her legendary. I was in my junior year and captain of the basketball team. I somehow made all-regional that year even though I still had not had my growth spurt and I was elected cheerleader—thanks to Joanna. It was during those football games that I missed her the most: the small figure trailing after the fabulous larger-than-life shadow. I never forgot that smile and her constant encouragement and counted us as lucky. She inspired me to believe in myself and to have confidence in my abilities. And she insisted that I take *can't* out of my vocabulary. I smiled at my elevated status: from mousy to super mouse. You can only do so much for some people, Joanna. *A tiny Texas town and a stranger that we claim as our legend.*

Chapter 19. Continuing Education & School of Hard Knocks

Tradition ruled when our higher education began in the fall of 1963. Libby and I did not venture beyond the predictable when deciding where to attend college. We had been accepted at the state college where both my parents and the Callaghans attended. I would study pre-law as I had planned since childhood. Dad had once suggested that I go with a big law firm in the city. I stubbornly refused to envision my future any other way than in practice with my dad. Not surprisingly, Mother thought it was a great idea to return home. She had not felt well for several years, and a cold realization was beginning to take hold. Her failing health was a continuing dilemma and perhaps an omen. She had dealt with high blood pressure for years without relief. The doctors were baffled. The prescribed medications seemed useless and did not lower the dangerously high numbers—180/100, 220/110, on and on. With the limited medical diagnostic procedures of the 60s, she had undergone radical exploratory surgery sliced from sternum to cervix to determine if there was some underlying cause not seen on the scans. Mother and Dad needed me—another reason to attend State within a couple of hours of home. I approached the change with less dread and a tinge of tempered excitement and optimism.

The excitement and beauty of that fall were destroyed instantly. We were on the brink of Thanksgiving break, and the dorm was abuzz with activity as the girls prepared for their holidays. The dorm was practically empty as we finished packing our bags for the long weekend. The television was blasting the exciting news about JFK and Jackie visiting Dallas, and then suddenly everything went dark. JFK and Governor Connally had been shot. We watched the news in stony silence listening for each word of what was to come, hesitating to take a breath. Then came the unbelievable horror that John F. Kennedy had been assassinated. It was a moment frozen in time with the lingering aftershock that could not be quieted. The memory of that day, where we were and what we were doing, and the accompanying disbelief remained with us as profound today as it was when it took place. It was the beginning of our Nation in the throes of the horror of assassination. We watched helplessly as one after another of our most brilliant and gifted leaders were cut down by spineless cowards. We became a country in chronic mourning, and our campus was no different. John F. Kennedy, Martin Luther King, Jr., and Robert Kennedy—our leaders, our crusaders, our future, loved and revered by the young—all cut down by assassins. These dark days blotted our world of hope and took years for our country to heal and overcome the nightmare.

As I continued my freshman year, I quickly learned that I was a sheltered, coddled and protected baby. I had felt better prepared to enter kindergarten. I was overcome by too many decisions. For the first time in my life, I was responsible for myself. Libby did not seem fazed. We settled into dorm life as roomies labeled as "independents" since we would not be joining a sorority. True to my nature, I convinced myself I was interested in my studies and wisely decided that my independent nature did not fit into the sorority lifestyle. Libby was not the least bit interested in becoming a sorority girl and dismissed most of them as privileged party girls without a brain or an original thought—definitely not her style. Whether I rejected sorority life because Libby did or because it did not fit into my overall goals, I never gave it a second thought. I would make my decision the right one. I was capable of creating my own social life and connections. As I look back, what a big nothing to obsess over. Many of the students who attended state college were recognized faces from ours and neighboring towns. The campus soon became familiar ground and took on the aspect of a large extension of high school, or it seemed so in my mind. But my heart was at home. College was a necessity to pursue my goals, not an escape from my hometown.

Our transition to college was not all smooth sailing, but our studies came naturally. We had disciplined study habits, so we were not intimidated by the advanced college courses. We attended our classes, studied for homework and tests, and turned in our classwork on schedule. The routine was actually pretty simple and being on my own gradually became natural and desirable rather than strange and unfamiliar. I went home almost every weekend, but Libby increasingly chose to stay and party over the weekends. She had not dated much in high school because she described the local boys as slim pickings and wimpy, and she was pretty sure there would be some exciting choices once in college. Her prediction proved to be correct and more than she was able to handle. She had her choice of guys and parties. She was busy.

During our second semester, she met a local boy who was in his second year, but not a sophomore—aptly described as a second-year freshman. I had not met him, but my radar easily detected reckless and trouble. She fell fast and hard. Everything he did or wanted to do exhilarated her. Libby believed the "big" party that Friday night was the party of the century rather than what it actually was—an all-night drunk. My appeal to reason that her behavior was risky and irresponsible fell on deaf ears. There was no talking her out of it. She was going. She would be expelled if caught. When Libby made up her mind, end of discussion. She methodically planned her escape out our dorm room after curfew and would not return until late Saturday night. Even though we were on the first floor, the drop out our window to the ground was at least ten to twelve feet. She timed the black and white security car as the campus police made their rounds. Then she carefully tied her sheet to the bedpost and lowered it out the window. I was amazed as she shimmied her way down the brick wall and jumped to the ground. She looked like a prison escapee. I watched as she ran full speed before the security car made its rounds, and then she disappeared into the darkness. As her accomplice, I took care of the evidence. I quickly gathered up the sheet, closed the window and said a prayer.

I worried for Libby and hoped she wouldn't get hurt. That was as far as I went; she had made it clear that she didn't want my help. I returned home most of my weekends to help my dad. Mother was spending less time in the office and was under the close watch of her doctors. Her blood pressure soared out of control. The doctors believed that her headaches and high blood pressure were associated with what they had now diagnosed as atherosclerosis or hardening of the arteries.

Our challenges during these four years extended beyond the classroom as we made our own decisions and faced the consequences. We were growing up. Libby had discovered boys and became party girl central. I coped with the illness of my mother and the ensuing complications. Libby's love life was not my pressing concern. I would be forced to grow up in a sudden and cruel way as life changed forever for my family and for me.

Chapter 20. Nella Claire Chastain

Nella Chastain was driving back to the office on a Wednesday afternoon after having her hair and nails done. She pulled in to park in front of the office dazed and confused. She barely recognized where she was. She did recognize that something was terribly wrong. She struggled to make her way out of the car. As she tried to step up to the curb, she stumbled and fell into a crumpled heap on the sidewalk and then blackness. Lorene saw her and yelled for John. Nella was unconscious.

Libby and I arrived at the hospital four hours later. Dad met us in the lobby. The news was not good. Mother had suffered a debilitating stroke and was in a coma. She was paralyzed on the right side. The doctors cautioned that it was too early to determine the extent and severity of the stroke, but the prognosis was bleak. The paralysis could be permanent and, because this stroke was so severe, she could die. I suddenly felt weak and faint and struggled to keep my balance. Libby tightened her arm securely around my waist. I methodically repeated to myself, "I must be strong" "I must be strong." My dad depended on me. I had never seen him so pale and lifeless. He looked like a stone statue. A sudden realization hit me like a brick. There was no buffer here. I was all he had.

"Oh, Dad, I have to see Mother. Can I go in now?"

"Yes, honey. I'll be in in a few minutes after I talk to the doctor."

The motionless form wrapped in white was hardly recognizable. There was medical equipment everywhere. Tubes and wires, IVs, ventilator, beeping monitors and oxygen flowing. This was a nightmare we were not prepared for. I searched desperately for a sign of comfort in this harsh, unfamiliar environment into which I had been thrust. Abruptly, I saw it. Mother's long, slender hand lay on the sheet; her freshly painted cherry red nails were perfectly manicured this very day. I knew Mother's schedule by heart. I smiled through the flow of hot tears. Wednesday was hair and nails day.

I clutched Mother's hand and bent over to kiss her on the cheek. "Mother, it's Claire. Daddy and I are here, and we love you so much. We won't leave you." Instantly, I caught the wonderful aroma of Mother's face powder. Instinctively, I recalled my first memory of going with her to the city department store. I saw her even now in the brown suit and coral blouse with her brown lizard pumps clicking on the store's marble floors. She took me by the hand and proudly led me to the cosmetics counter. I strutted my little self beside the beautiful woman with the striking red hair and green eyes. I looked up. She was the prettiest mother a girl could ever want. The concoctions had my head spinning as the aroma of the perfumes, creams and powders hit my nose and the splash of colors of lipsticks and rouges in every color and hue whether clear reds, bright oranges or vibrant pinks dazzled me making my head whirl.

The lady called her by name, "Oh, Nella, what a wonderful surprise. It's so good to see you, and I know this must be little Claire. I've heard so much about you, dear."

"Hello, Marie. Yes, Claire is excited for her first visit to the Cosmetics Department and to see you mix my powder."

"Of course. Claire, just remember you can't begin too young to take care of your skin. I'll be a moment, Nella, while I find your information."

The lady returned with her card file and produced a 3 x 5 index card. "Here is your formula. It won't take me but a few minutes."

She turned and used a small scoop to mix the creamy beige, pinks and even green and gold to make the perfect shade for my mother's flawless porcelain skin. The smell of the powder filled the air. When she was done, she carefully put the powder in a round white and gold box.

"Here, Nella. I have included some extra powder puffs." She handed my mother a crisp white paper bag with ribbons tied around it.

How many times had I seen my mother put the precious loose powder in its gold case compact? I would always cherish that day with my mother. I brought myself back. I felt guilty thinking such trivial thoughts in a crucial moment such as this.

I pulled up the stiff, black upright chair as close to Mother's bed as the equipment and nurses would allow. I tried to calm my rampant thoughts and focus on the reality before me. Mother was forty-eight years old. She lay comatose and perhaps dying. I turned as Dad came into the room. He softly laid his hand on my shoulder. "Honey, they are doing all they can. She is in good hands." Her dad's eyes were red and swollen. Tears flowed down her cheeks. Her helplessness overwhelmed her. This was a fall-to-your-knees moment with no relief in sight. I was drowning in the darkest depths of agony unable to ease our suffering. Mother lies before me now struggling to survive. Dad's anguish was too much for me to bear. I at once imagined that I felt as small and insignificant and helpless as a human could feel. I could do nothing but pray.

Undertow

I go to my knees for His strength in times of trouble,
turmoil and strife
To combat demons lurking, dragging me down
Mass of heavy darkness rising all around
Threatens to suffocate as I cling to hopeful life
To resurrect my struggling belief.
We call for his Spirit to lift and sustain
Against the raging current we cannot maintain
His sword of light will cut through the blackness
And calm the evil we cannot see.
Peaceful now and strong in our will
I hear His whisper to my soul: Be still.
Be strong in your Faith. Overcome with hope your
despair
Lay at His feet your burden of care.
And He will reflect his wondrous light.

Dad and I spent three nights with Mother in the hospital. On the fourth day, the doctors gave us the news that even though the damage from the stroke was extensive, with every passing day, the outlook was encouraging. The prognosis was cautionary. There was no way to assess the damage until she awoke from the coma which might be days or even weeks. When I look back, I wonder how we had the strength. You just do it. Our daily routine took on the customary schedule of vigil with loved ones in this situation. We took turns going home to shower, to eat, to try to rest. Lorene brought him the mail and any documents which needed his immediate attention. A constant stream of friends poured into the hospital to give their support. This was a time of not holding back. Friends and neighbors, business acquaintances, and church friends all reached out without hesitation. Everyone felt deeply for us and showed they cared in our moment of crisis. They offered their willingness and assurance of being there when we needed them and genuinely wanted to help ease our pain. We found comfort and strength in the arms of our friends. Insurance agent Jim Haggerty and his wife Millie were by our side every day for the first month. They came to the hospital regularly for the two-month duration of Mother's confinement to the hospital. She came out of the coma three weeks to the day after she suffered the stroke.

Her right side was completely paralyzed. Her speech was slurred and difficult to understand. She had no control of her bodily functions. Eventually, she was able to be lifted out of the bed into a chair for short periods. She needed to be cared for and tended to like a baby. The physical therapist came three times a day. The days and weeks blurred one into another until we realized we had to formulate a plan. It was decided that I must return to school. Dad would return to a part-time schedule at work. Mother's medical bills were astronomical. Dad and I discussed our options for her care which were few. He looked at several rehab places which were in the city, but he needed her close to him. He would care for her at home. We were lucky to find a vocational nurse who agreed to come five days a week eight hours a day. Dad and I would care for her on the weekends. We wanted her to have the best possible chance to recover. She was in the hospital for nine agonizing weeks.

We prepared to bring her home and set up a limited but functional physical therapy center on the screened-in porch. She had a pulley to exercise her arms and upper body, a half-bicycle that she pedaled from her wheelchair, a walker, a potty chair and hospital bed. She had to be lifted from her wheelchair to the potty chair and then back into her wheelchair or to a special recliner in the living room. It was an arduous daylight to daylight existence. She did not sleep well, and therefore my dad did not sleep. He functioned on the verge of physical and emotional exhaustion. Mother did her therapy and exercises trying her best to walk, but it was not to be. There had been too much irreversible damage. After months of using the walker and sliding the heavy metal leg brace, exhaustion and defeat took over. Her depression deepened once she realized she would not improve. Nella would never be the same, neither would we nor our lives. The piano stood gleaming, quiet and untouched. At that moment, I realized how much I adored her but had made few attempts to emulate her. My dreams from childhood revolved around my dad and being a lawyer. Truth be told, I was like my dad—gritty, stubborn, and headstrong. I looked up to my mother and perceived her as gentle and wise—qualities that seemed unattainable. Going forward, I would try to honor her by becoming like her.

To be sure, I had never dreamed of such an unthinkable tragedy. I thought, why not? Was I that arrogant or ignorant to think that our family's turn would not come to cope with crisis and tragedy? During these long months, I often thought about the greater pain other people have to face. I needed perspective to logically deal with what was happening to my family. What initially seemed unbelievable soon became routine. Everything revolved around taking care of Mother. That was all that Dad and I cared about.

The insurance company canceled her health insurance within a year, and no other company would insure her. Every expense was now out-of-pocket. Medical bills continued to climb. He and Mother had saved religiously for me to go to college, and Dad insisted that I must finish school. He was adamant that I make my best effort to clerk to earn money at one of the larger firms. I would have better opportunities offered to me—larger firms, larger cases and larger salary and bonuses. He went further. He did not think it was a good idea for me to plan to come home to practice law with him. He would continue his practice, but he did not foresee expanding it. There was no place for me. I was shattered; my dreams destroyed. All I heard was "Claire, you should begin to find your own way." I was beginning to wonder if I had added pressure on him rather than relieve it as had been my intentions. I suddenly realized I must focus on mapping out my own career and my own future. My little girl dreams were fantasy. *My dreams were not his dreams.*

I finished my last year of undergraduate studies and passed the Law School Admission Test, the LSAT. It should have been cause for celebration. I had taken another step on my way to seeing my dream fulfilled of becoming a lawyer. But mostly it was all a chore. Mother regained most of her memory and tried her best to recover the use of her right side but to no avail. Her speech did not improve. It was difficult for her to speak as well as difficult to understand her. Therefore, she seldom spoke other than a few sentences or phrases. She continued to use her days as productively as possible. She tried to read, but it was almost impossible for her to focus so someone would read to her. She filled her days doing her exercises and therapy and managed to show interest in a few television programs. Her true friends came to visit and to play Canasta occasionally. These friends were few. Many others either became too busy or no longer wanted to be bothered. Millie Haggerty was her best friend and remained loyal. She and Mother had worked in the same office for years, and both loved the Gardening Club and playing Canasta. Millie and Jim were their best couple friends. Millie was one of the few who did not abandon her and came to visit her often. Mother's physical limitations and after-stroke presence were too much for most people to handle. Trips out of the house were exhausting and increasingly rare. Her beautician came to the house to fix her hair and do her nails which she still seemed to enjoy. She hated being dependent but tolerated it with few complaints. She was the sweetest, easiest person to care for that a person could be. My mother was never demanding when well and sickness did not change that. She did her best with the cards dealt her.

As each Sunday afternoon approached and it was time for me to return to school, I went into the bathroom and just bawled my eyes out. It was increasingly difficult for me to leave her. The upside down, inside out turmoil and emotional rawness of our lives became the new norm. Sometimes Lorene came to the house to work so that Dad could stay home with Mother. He constantly dictated into the Dictaphone giving Lorene instructions on the pleadings and correspondence and the phone calls to make. I was struck by the sheer volume of work that he and

Mother accomplished. Lorene had stepped in as a substitute for Mother, but she was a poor replacement. I understood Dad had to have someone to help him. His law practice was at stake. The law business is all about deadlines. Timeliness in the law is akin to Godliness. Missing deadlines or appearances is unforgivable and not tolerated. Arrangements had to be made with either the court or opposing counsel to get hearings and other appearances scheduled and rescheduled.

Dad and Lorene were the new team, and a new receptionist was hired. I struggled to accept the changes as positive. But try as I might, I resisted. I felt pushed out, tossed aside and resentful. My heart ached for my mother and for me. The isolation I felt was surely minuscule compared to how my mother must feel. The changes in many ways seemed natural and part of what was necessary. But that did not mean I had to like them. It was Lorene twenty-four hours a day, every day. She was bold and intrusive. Her brazen attitude made me wonder: where did she come from? I don't mean the obvious. I mean credentials before she took over the receptionist desk in my parents' office. I had a passing thought that it might be worthwhile to ask some questions about Miss Lorene. She was too available and too attentive for my liking. *Barracuda circling.*

The last year of college was a blur. With constant studying to make up classes and preparing for the LSAT, with the cooperation and understanding of my professors, I graduated in August 1967 and was ready to begin three years of law school. Libby had joined the Peace Corps. She would go to field school and then be assigned to Costa Rica to teach. Her dreams were coming true. While we struggled to keep our lives in check with some semblance of order and stability, change on the verge of revolution and chaos continued to rule in the world. Vietnam was raging, and true to war and particularly this war, there were no winners.

Chapter 21. Our Vietnam Warrior

The news of Seth's death was heart-wrenching. I had barely got to know him, and now he had been taken from us. Why had I waited so long to get to know my cousin? He might have been older than I, but all I remembered was I found something else to do when I had the chance to be with the Callaghans. With Libby in Costa Rica, it was my place to go to the Ranch and see Aunt Angela and Uncle Evan. Besides I wanted to be with them. I was proud of Seth. When you said exceptional, you were talking about Seth Callaghan. He was good at everything he did, and people loved his easygoing way. He liked people, and they knew it. He naturally attracted people and made them feel like they knew him.

The loss of our brave warriors continued to be devastating even in our small town. When Seth was taken from us, I tried to phone Libby as soon as I heard, but the phone connections to Costa Rica were horrible, and I never reached her. Somehow the Callaghans got through and had already talked to her. They all decided that, as badly as she insisted on coming home, it was too much to ask since she had been with the Peace Corps such a short while. She would not be here for Seth's funeral. As I drove to the Ranch, I saw Seth's airplane in the hangar. I remembered his mother once said to him that it seemed flying was his whole life. He gently corrected her saying, "Mom, I know you don't understand why I love flying so much. All I can say is that flying makes my life whole."

It was a period of change and turmoil in our Nation that touched us all. The cruelty of war further split and fractured a country struggling with tragedy of every kind imaginable and monumental change. The news was filled with burning and looting, protests, civil rights and integration, assassinations and an epidemic of mass and serial killings. It seemed the black cloud of Vietnam loomed over every family. Seth had been accepted into Officer Candidate School, then fixed wing and helicopter school. He had spent two years training for his assignment. Ordinarily, such dedication would be reason for celebration, but Evan and Angela did not feel they had cause to celebrate. They did not support the war and definitely did not want their son in a helicopter—reduced to a sitting duck to be shot down. Vietnam was raging, and Seth had made his decision. He had chosen to go into the service and to fly a helicopter.

Their youngest son had a mind of his own and would not be talked out of it. He felt strongly about both aspects of his upcoming tour of service—a chance to fly and a chance to serve his country. He shared a limited amount of information about his upcoming tour. Evan and Angela tried to be supportive and encouraging, but it was impossible to pretend that they supported the war. Seth insisted it was his obligation. He would not stand by while his peers did the dirty work. He was able-bodied and willing to serve his country. He tried to reassure his parents that he was doing the right thing. The war had intensified in recent months and casualties mounted. As the war dragged on, the controversy raged over our involvement in it and was splitting our country apart. The nightly news carried graphic reports each day of the battles being fought along with a continuing tally of casualties and injured. Families held their breaths hoping against hope that the fateful news would not be that their loved one's unit was among the day's casualties. The Callaghans were not bashful about their position on Vietnam. They did not buy the argument that we were fighting the spread of Communism by the Viet Cong. Sadly, future events would bear out the ugly truth. The ultimate "Peace Treaty" was our respectable way out after ten years of catastrophic losses leaving the Viet Cong to take over. Vietnam was destined to be a Communist country.

Seth was assigned to the Helicopter Assault Tactics. After completing his training, he served fifteen months. His helicopter was shot down on November 19, 1968. He was buried in the family cemetery on the Ranch next to his grandfather Edmond Seth Callaghan who served during World War I with the Army Air Corps in France. Vietnam dragged on for over twenty years at a cost that is still staggering:

Estimates range as high as two to three million total lives lost. Evan and Angela were shattered by their loss, but they did not hide the pride bursting forth out of their sorrow. Their son had given his life serving his country. Vietnam claimed lives cruelly and indiscriminately as any war does. The Callaghans were adamantly opposed to Seth going to Vietnam, but his legacy of service and sacrifice had left an indelible though bittersweet mark.

The Callaghans were determined to honor their son's memory. They wanted to combine their love of having children on the Ranch and helping children who would welcome that opportunity. Libby's idea of starting a summer program with a local orphanage had been put on hold. Evan was simply too short-handed for a new venture. After Seth's death and with Libby on assignment, the opportunity was ideal to move ahead with the plan. Ian was working on the Ranch fulltime and taking on the majority of the day-to-day ranch work. The bunkhouse would accommodate sixteen kids, and each group could stay on the Ranch two weeks. That way, over ten weeks in the summer, they could have a total of 80 kids. Angela began the project by contacting the orphanage to see if there was an interest in such a program. John Chastain drew up the legal papers. Camp Callaghan Kids was becoming a reality. Evan saw his wife come alive with a new purpose and enthusiasm. The bunkhouse needed some work and a new shingle: *Seth's Rangers.*

Angela had procrastinated as long as she could with good conscience. She fought her reluctance to go through Seth's belongings and her thoughts of violating his privacy. She gave in and reached for the one thing that beckoned her attention knowing full well that it was the one thing she would regret having done so. It was a letter from Erin to Seth.

April 14, 1967

Dear Seth:

This is the hardest thing I have ever had to do. I have put off writing this hoping that something would happen to change my mind. I know that you are committed to your assignment in Vietnam and there is nothing I can or want to say or do to try and change that. I admire your courage and selflessness and love you with all my heart for it, putting your own life in jeopardy for your country. I have wrestled with this decision and thought about the consequences. There is no turning back.

As you know, I had previously been engaged, and he has come back into my life. We have set a date to get married this summer. I hesitated to tell you in a letter, but I didn't want you to be under a false impression once you returned. I know it sounds selfish of me, but I hope you will understand and forgive me.

You are in my thoughts and prayers. Stay safe and may God Bless.

Erin

Seth had never mentioned the breakup with Erin, but a mother knew. Angela had seen a difference in Seth—a single-minded intensity and focus on serving in Vietnam. It was uncharacteristic of him in so many ways. He loved to make plans for the future. Yes, he needed to be focused going to Vietnam, but the Seth she knew would be planning for the day when he came home. There was never a word about what Seth planned after his tour of duty. It was as if, Angela shuddered to think, he had thrown caution to the wind. He had given everything he had to give.

Chapter 22. Jurisprudence

Deferments. A dirty word to some but, for most given a choice, going to school was preferable to going to war. When I walked into my first class of law school, my first thought, how many lawyers does the world need? My law school class was bulging much like an overfed squire on the verge of popping the buttons on his vest. That in itself was cause for concern. I questioned further, even if a large percentage of us don't pass the Bar, how in the name of Oliver Wendell Holmes will we all find jobs? The class was pretty much composed of characters you find in the outside world. It had its rightful share of windbags, know-it-alls, heritage lawyers as in, it's my family tradition, my daddy/brother/uncle/cousin is a lawyer (maybe you've heard of him), three-piece suits who were well-connected and had their eyes on the big firms and the big bucks. Then there were a few of us who were pretty ordinary law students with good grades, high goals and unrealistic ideals who genuinely wanted and expected to be good lawyers. In spite of some of the negative perceptions, I still regarded the law as a respected profession. I looked up to my dad as the ultimate I aspired to be—esteemed, dedicated and hard-working.

I was lucky that I had no other outside distractions except for what was happening at home with my mother. That was all-encompassing. Law school was my diversion. I spent most of my hours in the law library. There were some classmates who were not as fortunate. They had to juggle jobs, spouses and children, money worries—all competing for their attention. Class time was filled with introductory courses, substantive law, the Texas court system, and beginning statute and case law research. Many of my classmates were doing pro bono work as interns, but I needed to earn money. I had applied to work in the summers for firms that had registered with the school who employed student law clerks. I interviewed with a medium-sized firm downtown who specialized in civil litigation and corporate law. It was way too early for me to decide what kind of law I would practice, but the law firm experience would be a requirement to get my foot in the door of a good firm. I did not have the luxury of being picky. I needed to work for a firm that would pay me.

The first summer I worked closely with LouAnn one of the large case litigation paralegals. Law school may have provided the tools, but I learned my basic litigation skills working in the law firm war room. I began to realize how much I had to learn from the basics of how to analyze and prepare a case file for trial to the complex responsibilities of how to develop a case; investigation and interviewing witnesses; obtaining and analyzing records and documents, and identifying and securing expert witnesses. I attended depositions to observe the attorneys in action and was given the responsibility of reviewing the case and providing areas of inquiry for use by the lead attorneys.

By the second year, I was confident that I had made a good career choice. I had made a new friend and, with Libby in the Peace Corps, that was a surprise bonus. LouAnn had been a litigation paralegal for twelve years and ran circles around most of the newbie lawyers. She was confident, efficient and experienced and could be handed a new case file and run with it with minimum direction from the attorneys assigned to the case. And talk about detailed. Not the slightest minutiae escaped her. Attorneys may have supervised her work, but she carried a great deal of the burden of working the case. Working with her directly gave me a wealth of experience particularly in developing a case and preparing a case for trial. As I began my second summer with the firm, our relationship changed as we became personal friends. She was someone I confided in and, with all the changes and stresses in my life, I needed a friend close at hand.

I met Michael Levy my second year of law school. We had several classes together the first year but only exchanged casual glances and greetings. We were running into each other at the law library since we were in the same research class. Our friendship began somewhere in the law library amid countless volumes of Vernon's statutes and the Civil

Practice and Remedies Code as we struggled to understand and apply what we read to write our research papers. He was easygoing and smart and much better than I at understanding all the legal mumbo jumbo and a blessing in disguise. Otherwise, I doubtless would have struggled all the way out the door of law school. One thing was clear—the law is not a profession for the lazy.

I continued to go home as often as possible. Mother had a series of small strokes and was bedridden. She rarely spoke and barely acknowledged visitors. She managed a crooked smile for Dad and me, but we failed to spark her interest. We were losing her. I saw her continue to deteriorate; she was losing her will to live. Dad confided that he could no longer keep her at home and had decided to move her to the local nursing home. Those were the dreaded words I prayed not to hear, but I understood it was inevitable. Two aides had been needed for the last few months for her care, the cooking and cleaning. It was too much for my dad. It had been three long, agonizing years since the stroke.

My first visit to the nursing home was as dismal as I expected. I quietly knocked then entered a small, square stark white room with a hospital bed, black vinyl recliner and television, an occasional chair, table and lamp. A few hanging clothes and Mother's robe hung in the closet along with shelves for pillows and blankets and a built-in chest of drawers for Mother's few belongings. It was sparse, white and cold. I set down the small glass bowl of daisies on the table.

"Mother, look at the pretty daisies. I know they are your favorite."

Her mother reached out her good hand and attempted a crooked smile. I clasped her hand and kissed her gently on the cheek. There was no familiar scent of face powder or rouge, no creamy beautiful lips, just antiseptic. There didn't seem to be anything important enough to talk about. Claire tried a few sentences of small talk about law school but then abruptly stopped and sat quietly holding her mother's hand. Her mother's eyes closed and the tears bubbled up and seeped through her eyelids and onto her cheeks. Now words fail and even get in the way. Our time on earth together was coming to an end. Forcing small talk about inconsequential nothings was a morbid waste.

Claire leaned over and held her mother close. "I love you, my precious mother, more than anything in this world. You are the best mother anyone could ever have. Thank you for all you have done for me. You have given me so much."

She smoothed her beloved mother's strands of red and gold and kissed her perfect cheek. She whispered, "You are the woman, wife and mother that I pray to be." She realized it would not be long now.

Two months later on May 19, Nella Claire Chastain died from another massive stroke. Her suffering was over. The church overflowed with many people having to stand outside. People loved and respected Nella. She had lived here most of her life and had served the community personally and professionally. I stood tall and straight as Mother taught me. I seemed to throw off my self-pity as if it were an outer garment. I refused to let my sorrow consume me. I walked straightway into the crowd instead of away from it, my head held high and my shoulders back. I shook every hand with a smile thanking them for their support and kindness during my mother's illness. I was filled with pride that Nella Claire Chastain was my mother and that I was her daughter. How fortunate I had been throughout my life to have her as my guardian angel.

At the cemetery, I stayed until the last shovel of earth covered Mother's grave. Then I laid three perfect white daisies on top of the mound. During Mother's illness, I had often tried to envision life without her. I could not. I prayed for strength for Dad and me as we faced the coming dark days. The future towered before me like a brick wall. I no longer had my mother's physical presence, but I took comfort that her strong spirit would never leave me. Mother would always be with me; and she would encourage me to take one step at a time. Long ago, even before she became ill, I remembered Mother saying a strange thing which made no sense to me until now, "There will be occasions in your life when putting one foot in front of the other will be your major task for the day."

Law school was a welcome way to lose myself in work as a diversion that did not make me feel guilty. It was a constant battle to not give in to the heavy weight of sadness and loss. I was thankful to have Michael and LouAnn by my side. They gave me friendship, support and understanding when I needed it the most. He and I were studying for finals when he caught me by surprise.

He wanted to take me out for breakfast. He asked if I liked deli and I was confused, "You mean…deli for breakfast?"

"Well, it will be brunch. I know a great place with the best nosh in town."

"Sure. That sounds great." We drove a few miles from the campus and pulled in to park at an old house with a huge wraparound porch and a few tables outside.

"Let's sit outside this morning. The weather is pretty good today, at least for Texas." He grinned.

"Sure. I'd like that."

"Here, let's sit over there." He pointed to the last table. "I'll go order our food. You'll just have to trust me on this one."

In a few minutes, he returned with a large tray and the most delicious sampling of bagels, lox, pastries, cream cheese and fruit that I had ever seen. "Dig in. Hope you enjoy it."

It was the first of many times together grabbing a quick bite or an occasional movie. We were taking it slow. There were a limited number of hours in a day, and we had already obligated most of them. We were committed to our goals. We enjoyed getting acquainted and being together, although initially, we didn't have much in common outside the law. He had graduated from Temple University. His dad had been transferred to New Jersey when he was a kid, and they had recently moved back to Texas. He wanted to stay here to practice law and liked Texas with one proviso—our weather and well, maybe, our accents. He made no bones about it. He jokingly described both as oppressive and uncivilized. He doubted he would ever get used to either.

I looked at him quizzically. "Really, Michael. You think we get used to the heat and to you Yankees? It's not nice to come into our south 40 and make fun of the way we talk, youse guys."

We were different, but it didn't seem to matter. We enjoyed each other's company and our future in the law was our connection. I was focused on law school, but in the back of my mind, I realized change was in the air at home. The phone call came from my dad that I both dreaded and knew that was overdue. He wanted me to come home and help him go through Mother's belongings. Her closet remained as it had for years, organized and efficient, and untouched. Rows of high heels in black patent, brown leather, white spectator pumps, espadrilles and flats with matching handbags lined the shelves. Mother loved clothes and wore them so well. The suits she wore to work with coordinating silk blouses were covered in plastic bags. Everything was meticulously organized. That was my mother's way—efficiency as a time saver but without sacrifice of style. *Très chic.* When you look at that closet, you see these clothes belonged to someone who cared.

Dad glanced at me and smiled, "Your mother had great taste. I can remember her wearing every piece of clothing in here and how wonderful she looked. Someone will get good use of these things."

He was doing the right thing to donate her clothing, but the process was pure torture. Just get through this, Claire, I kept repeating in my head.

"Is there anything of hers you want?" he asked, as he slid the hangers over the rod.

I thought for a minute to be polite but knew instantly. "Her brown lizard high heels and handbag."

I wanted more and felt I was entitled. What about her jewelry? Then there was the land. She had inherited the family home place from her parents. Granted, it was not thousands of acres, but it had value to our family and particularly to my mother and me.

During mother's illness, she had made a strange request. She had asked how I was doing in law school and was particularly interested in whether I had studied deeds and contracts. Then she asked me to draw up the necessary papers (warranty deed) transferring her property to me.

"Mother, I am…have you and Dad discussed this?" I was aghast and caught totally off guard. I always assumed that the acreage would be included in her will, and I also assumed my dad was her sole beneficiary.

"Claire, I've caught you by surprise, I know, but this is important to me. I have always wanted you to have the land. I should have taken care of this before I became ill."

I was trying to collect my thoughts. "Shouldn't we have Dad draw up the papers?"

"No, I don't want confrontation and conflict which you know I need to avoid. This is what I want, and this is between you and me. Help me, please. I cannot rest until I know this matter is settled."

My heart was breaking. I wanted to abide by her wishes. But I felt a heavyweight of betrayal. What would my dad think? Never in my wildest dreams did I picture my mother asking me and not my dad to fulfill her last request. In my heart, this scenario was more complicated than a transfer of deed. I was torn.

Mother sensed my apprehension. "Claire, I know this is not easy for you. But it's my last hope. Maybe someday you will build the dream house next to your field of wildflowers. I know you are the one who can understand how important this is to me." She smiled faintly and beckoned me to her. She knew I understood all of it.

Now the question was, how do I tell my dad that I have an executed (though not recorded) deed signed by my mother? He was going to be upset and feel betrayed and accuse me of using undue influence on my mother. As a wise lawyer, he would advise that Mother was ill and wasn't capable of making such decisions. His final statement would be: it would be tough or impossible to uphold the transfer in court. Maybe I should not ever mention it. My lazy side kicked in. Why cause a ruckus? The timing definitely was not right. But when would it ever be?

Suddenly, I jerked back to the present. I never questioned him about her Will out of respect. I did not want to appear crass or money-grubbing. My daydreaming was cut short when he started to speak. I hoped he would mention her Will and discuss what she wanted to happen to her possessions. That would be a perfect moment to mention her land. But there was nothing.

He must have heard my thoughts. "Claire, your mother had a small life insurance policy with you as the beneficiary. It will come in handy to pay for your expenses until you get through law school. Also, I want you to have your mother's jewelry, and I know she would have wanted that, too."

"Dad, I appreciate that so much. It means the world to me." I hugged him and fought back the weakness of tears.

I was struggling. "Don't hold back, dear Claire, I know how much you loved and admired your mother. Trust me, the feeling was absolutely mutual. You were her pride and joy."

There was another practical reason for clearing out the house. Dad and Lorene were getting married. I was not shocked or even slightly surprised. They had become a couple even before Mother was cold in her grave. I tried to remind myself that he had a right to be happy and not be alone. What would be a respectable amount of time? That was not the worst of it. She was moving into my mother's house. Life goes on, Claire, I reminded myself. I went to the wedding at the house—it was all so nice and polite—I did not make a scene, just my usual smiling, accepting self. Inside, I was seething. I decided it was because of the woman he chose. I was not against him remarrying. I did not like Lorene. She snapped her tentacles into my dad way too soon to be respectable, long before my mother made her exit. I may be young, but I am a woman, and I know a schemer. Lorene had planned this. Nevertheless, my feelings and opinions were not solicited by either side. I had to do my best to make the best of it. Life had played a dirty trick on Claire. Life had turned into a bad dream.

Chapter 23. Michael Levy

It was my last summer as a law clerk and my first experience working on a case when trial was a real possibility. My full attention was on a rollover case against an auto manufacturer with potential damages nearing a million dollars. LouAnn and I had boxes of medical records and documents to organize and summarize and trial notebooks to prepare. Depositions still had to be summarized and documents copied. With a scheduled trial date in the fall, we were working long days into night and most weekends. LouAnn was lining up several expert witnesses, contacting our eyewitnesses and getting subpoenas served. The court had ordered mediation, but so far no agreement had been reached. The lawyers had instructed us to proceed as usual: prepare and plan for trial. During all this whirlwind of activity, Michael had invited me to a family summer outing at their lake house. I wanted to go desperately, but I had to say no.

"Claire, I understand. Your work comes first. We will go another weekend, I promise. Hopefully, just you and I will have some quiet time together." He kissed me lightly but held me tightly. I looked up into his dark brown eyes and instantly was lost in his good looks. Maybe just maybe…no, back to reality. I could not afford to be self-indulgent right now. There was no need to add complications.

Michael and I agreed. We were ready to get school behind us and pass the Bar. The hours of constant research, boring cases involving either big insurance companies or corporations, and writing never-ending memos of law had taken its toll. So far, the law had not been the least bit exciting or even rewarding. I questioned whether I was ready to sign up for a lifetime of a repeat of the same. I was also horrified at the thought: might it be that my lifelong quest of being a lawyer was going to be just another boring job? Neither one of us knew where our passions lie or what our specialty of law would be. Basically, we were lost souls looking for a sign—this way to a rewarding law career. One thing was for sure. We were ready to put school behind us and go to work.

A strange thing had happened during these law school years. I had begun questioning my career choice. But I wondered about Michael and whether he had become disenchanted with the law. One day in the law library we looked at each other and knew. I had experienced my first taste of trial law. LouAnn and I spent months preparing the big case for trial, and thirty days from the scheduled trial date (which had been reset too many times to count), the parties settled. Okay, so that is not all bad, our clients (and the firm) get their money, but it is definitely a downer to me. The courtroom is theater for lawyers. Excuse me if I sound disrespectful or even vulgar, it's the ultimate in theatrics. You prepare your case, you practice in front of the mirror and in mock court, you use all your resources to win. It's the adversarial battlefield. Trial lawyers thrive on the competition of presenting and winning their cases—it's all about victory for *you* and your client and defeating the other side. I was having difficulty picturing me as one of many worker bee lawyers in a firm of giants where workdays less than sixteen hours were frowned upon and the chances of getting the desirable cases where you are recognized and making partner in twenty years were slim to none. Without pretense, I laid it out to Michael. He hung on my every word. He never showed one iota of disapproval, surprise or disbelief.

When I was done, he said, "Maybe that is part of what law school is all about, Claire—discovery of a different kind."

"Don't get me wrong, Michael. I still want to be a lawyer. I just don't want to join all the rats."

Michael smiled. "I agree."

Claire was stunned. "What are you saying?"

Michael carefully chose his words. "I think we have options once we pass the Bar. There will be a downside. There are no guarantees. The money will be uncertain and not as good initially. We have to build our clientele. This option definitely has risks. We would be building our own business. I think we've got what it takes to make it on our own. It will take a lot of hard work and sacrifice but so will working for someone else. We might as well invest in ourselves from the beginning."

He took a breath. "We definitely need a break and finals are coming up. A trip to the lake house will do us both a lot of good." Michael looked at me intently but not waiting for my response. "No excuses. We're going."

He stepped toward me and pulled me to him in one soft, slow, comforting motion. "We need alone time, Claire." I looked up, and his soft, full lips were on mine. The weekend looked promising. I was allowing myself the luxury of emotions and caring for Michael. I knew it was risky behavior but overdue.

As we pulled under the lake house to park, I saw instantly this was no ordinary lake cabin. The outside stairs led to a screened-in porch with an unobstructed view of the lake beyond. The large grassy yard sloped down to a boat dock housing an 18' ski boat and fishing pier. Lounge chairs for sunning and just kicking back lined the wood dock. On the side of the house under the shade of two large oaks, there was another outdoor living area—a large patio with a grill and outdoor kitchen, dining table and chairs. This place invited you to have fun and relax without a care in the world. Inside there were three bedrooms and three baths, kitchen, living and dining area enclosed with wall-to-wall windows overlooking the lake.

"I've been coming here ever since I was a tadpole. My grandparents bought this place back in the 40s and we have had family outings and vacations here ever since. This is my runaway. Let's make it our hideaway."

I felt his energy; Michael had big plans for us. He was full of surprises. He put his hand in his pocket and pulled out a small white box. "I hope you like it. It was my grandmother's." I starred at the incredibly gorgeous two-carat emerald cut diamond. I could not take my eyes off my left-hand's third finger sparkling brilliantly in the light.

"Oh, Michael. It is the most magnificent ring I've ever seen but do you realize what you are doing? I haven't even met your parents."

"You will tonight. We are going to dinner at their favorite restaurant. So wear something red. You know you're irresistible in red. I hope they are prepared to be swept off their feet. I say we shoot our full load."

"What are you talking about?" I was beyond confused.

He drew me closer. "We're engaged, and we are going to be law partners. I want us to build a *complete* life together."

"That might be too much for your parents. This is our first meeting. You know we have—well, so many details to work out."

"In due time, little lady. Let's enjoy the moment. Reality and religion later."

"I have told them all about you. They know how crazy I am about you. We are going to be partners in life both personal and professional. Careful kid, this might be serious." He winked and then held me close against him. He would not be the first to let go. I was happier than I ever thought possible. I was free falling in my own outer terrestrial limits— *Stardust.*

Michael went over to the stereo and punched the right button. Our favorite song, *Deep Purple,* began to play. He reached for me and held me close. I floated in his arms, but my mind was twirling with lingering doubts. I struggled with the mental clutter threatening to darken my blissful moment.

A gnawing realization: he is Jewish. I have no intentions to convert. How could this relationship work? Sooner or later, we would have to face this impasse. I had a sinking feeling this relationship if not doomed was severely compromised. *Practical reality versus romantic illusion. Another fantasy bites the dust.*

Chapter 24. Lorene

Dad and Lorene set up house in my mother's house. I had been home twice since they married six months ago. It looked small of me, but I would not accept her moving in and taking over my mother's place in her house. She got all new furniture for the living room and their bedroom. The red Formica table and chairs where we ate every meal, spent countless hours playing games and having family conferences was the first to go. I resented her disposal of our memories. How many hours were spent at that table? We talked and discussed, sat silently and contemplated, laughed and cried, did homework, drew up house plans and planned family vacations. Hey, Claire, those are just things my good sense echoed. Nonsense. Possessions are so much more than mere things. They are our family heritage; they hold and ignite our memories, signal moments and give us pause for reflection; ground us with reality—trigger points. I grew up around that table. Serious talks and family discussions, as well as fun, games and laughter, were embodied in that Formica. I was as mad as the table was red. What nerve of that woman to bulldoze her way through our home. It all signaled her lack of respect for my mother and me and our family.

Dad and Lorene had already been on two long, expensive trips in contrast to my mother who dreamed and hoped to go to Hawaii once she felt they had the extra money and the time was right. Mother was practical and helped Dad keep a tight rein on spending. Naturally, Lorene was not that concerned since she was spending money made off the backs of my mom and dad's hard work and sacrifice. She dressed in the finest designer dresses and shoes although before John Chastain she was accustomed to looking well-dressed and well-groomed. Clearly, that was no longer good enough for her. She made periodic shopping trips to the city and added another large walk-in closet to hold all her fabulous finds. Her blonde hair never saw a dark root thanks to weekly trips to the salon and monthly trips to the city for professional cuts.

"The hairdressers at Coif'd Style are hair stylists, not barbers like around here. Claire, you should get a nice haircut. You will be amazed at how manageable your hair will be," she wisely advised. Now she was an expert on hair.

"Maybe I will after I get a job. Right now, my haircut is the least of my priorities."

I never heard my dad complain except in jest one evening at dinner. He and Lorene had just come home from a trip to Europe. Dad was explaining that the cost of the trip was minor. It was Lorene's shopping tab in France and Italy that nearly sent him over the edge. She was flaunting a new diamond and ruby ring and an 18kt gold bracelet among her other indulgences. I was not privy to my dad's finances, but he was not wealthy. With Lorene's penchant for spending, it would not take her long to turn him into a pauper.

I had to come to grips with my bad feelings and the continuing dilemma of why Lorene bothered me. I was intent on getting to the bottom of it all. She had worked for my parents for what seemed many years before my mother died. She was not from here. Mother had talked Dad into hiring a receptionist to help her with the phone and the overflow typing and office work. I didn't want to ask Dad or Lorene and arouse their suspicion, but I wondered where she came from and who hired her and when exactly. I was a kid too busy running amuck to have paid much attention then. It seemed she had pretty much been in their office for as long as I remembered.

Maybe Michael or LouAnn would have some ideas on how to check out Lorene. If nothing else, it would set my mind at ease. There was a nagging voice that truly wanted my dad to be happy. If that meant letting some blonde bimbo march through his assets like Sherman through Georgia, then fine. She was not as old as my parents, but she was not young either. Where was her family? Had she been previously married or have any children? I had never heard my dad mention Lorene's background. Maybe he didn't have a clue either. What was obvious is that Lorene was ready and waiting for my dad on the rebound before he gathered his wits after Mother's long illness and death. I was certain that Lorene had been on a mission. She patiently waited until the right moment to execute her plan precisely on target. Her timing was impeccable. All those months I watched her, she was symmetry in motion. She never made a misstep or missed an opportunity. She was there whenever or wherever John Chastain needed her personally or professionally. She had successfully edged me out. She had isolated and seduced my dad into her web, a retreat from his sad, stressful existence with Mother and me.

I needed a rest from this continuing melodrama. I had received a letter from Libby and had stuffed it hurriedly into my purse. I retrieved it now and saw that it was even more crumpled than when I had gotten it out of the mailbox and barely readable. I guess they handle the mail from Costa Rica a lot before it reaches the party to whom it is intended. Anyway, I looked forward to her letters and definitely needed a break:

June 26, 1969

Dear Claire:

This is long overdue, I know. My life has changed so much that I hardly know where to begin. I have slowly and painfully, I might say, learned some basic Spanish although I have far to go. But it has not slowed me down one bit with the students. These children have such a wide-eyed innocence and yearning to learn that they let nothing stand in their way, even a language barrier. They continue to inspire and amaze me. I learn much more from them than they do from me. I truly believe that with constant war and unrest, hard work and dedication to helping others is the way most of us can contribute to making the world a better and peaceful place.

Our living conditions are basic—okay maybe that's a stretch depending on the comparison. It is astonishing how little we actually need. I am well, get plenty to eat and have my basic needs met. I thrive on what I am doing, so I don't spend my days wishing for things I do not have. What I do miss is you, my closest and dearest friend. I think of you daily and of course, beat myself up for not being with you during these tough times. I know you know that my heart is with you always. Always remember—I can be there in a few hours thanks to living in the fabulous jet age. San José, the capital, is a few hours from here.

I am learning every day, and it is overwhelming. The women here are amazing and have taken me under their wing. I am learning to weave! The rugs and handmade textiles are absolute works of art. My handiwork is nothing to compare with theirs, but I am proud to learn a new skill. They are so patient and understanding, I know now what it means to adapt to a new culture.

Your letters mean so much. Who would have ever thought our love of writing would take this direction? We are back to old-fashioned letter writing—who does that anymore? Just send a quick greeting card that someone else has already done all the work and written the prose which is just perfect for any occasion—whatever it is.

*You and I have often talked about **the** goal in life—to live a life of meaning and substance. Well, now I know that is not as easy as it sounds. Some of us may search a lifetime trying to feel like something in a world that seems to thrive on making people feel like nothing. After all, is said and done, we agreed that life is a journey and there has to be more than center court or center stage. At this point, I believe that I am on the right track. When I first volunteered, I felt I was running away from my problems. But this has turned out to be the most rewarding and fulfilling experience I hoped for.*

I will volunteer another two years and spend some of my R & R working with the people here. There is so much to do. We are building houses, and they need as many hands as they can get. In a way, I hesitate to return to the States because I know I will be tempted to stay. I do hope to come home at the end of my next assignment. We will have so much to talk about. I can't wait to meet Michael. I know you two will make a success of your partnership. You've always wanted to be a lawyer, and you will be the best. Keep to your goals, girl!

You've got to know, my dear friend, that I have changed. Much of this you already know since you know me better than I know myself. It's clear to me now that I have continued to allow my childhood struggles to weigh me down and suffocate the light within. I was addicted to carrying a load I could not sustain. The preoccupation with that load provided a convenient vehicle of immobility. I could remain stagnant with a clear conscience: my built-in inability to move forward. Once my family was torn apart, I began to realize that the strength and comfort I frantically searched for would not come from the Callaghans or my friends or any other human being.

As a small child, I held tight to my belief that everything would be all right someday and did not worry about tomorrow. Mother said that God would take care of us and would always be with us. Through our hardship, I began to question whether that was true and became hardened to the idea that God was looking after us. Then I decided since nothing else was working and things were becoming progressively worse for our family, it must be up to me to fix things. I decided to take on the Lord's load. Somehow the idea entered my head that we were not doing enough to help ourselves and that was the reason for my family's plight. During that process, my child's faith was destroyed. I began my new life at age ten with a shattered spirit and dead soul.

Adoption fixed many economic problems. I had everything a child needed or wanted materially—food, shelter, clothing, education and opportunities— even the intangibles of security and hope. But I was dead inside. It was many years before I conceded that there was one way that I could become whole again. I at once acknowledged that God had provided the solution to our family. I accepted that it was not a perfect outcome. But at last I confessed my selfishness to want everything as I thought it should be. Yes, we had to give up our family. But we were blessed to have a second chance at life through the Grace of God, the Chastains, the Callaghans and all the families who stepped in to embrace and love us. There was an awakening in me. I acknowledged that I was foolhardy to think that I was or ever could be in control. It was a hard road. I stubbornly held tight to my lofty, arrogant ideals of my own power until I accepted Him and the acceptance of my weak human limitations. I learned to be thankful and to accept the love others offered me.

One thing you can be sure of, as my world has broadened, Libby's importance has diminished. That is a good thing I think, and I hope that is some (if not all) of what this adventure is about.

Let's just say that we both must move forward and leave it at that. I know you understand without explanation.
My love to you dear Claire.

In my prayers always,
Libby

I cried for her. I knew her struggle and longing to be a whole person. I loved her, but I could only do so much. To know that she has come to peace and understanding and renewal filled me with such exuberant hope—for her and for us all. She had shared so much with me over the years about her past, but it was long and painstaking. It meant opening all the old wounds. The fact that she confided in me in a letter I felt was a great sign of her progress.

Libby's letters always made me feel better. It lessened the task of facing my realities with Lorene. I needed Libby's support and no-nonsense common sense about now. I was thankful for the support I did have. Michael and LouAnn did their best to understand me in this situation with Lorene.

They understood my concerns although I got the feeling they were holding back. They thought I was being paranoid, jealous and resentful. Michael put aside his judgmental feelings and suggested that a background check be done on Lorene and LouAnn agreed. She had contacts but she could get into real trouble for using her sources. Those people and the tools for getting records were strictly for law firm cases and not to be used for her friends' problems. Michael wanted to help me pay for the investigative report on Lorene. He would hire the private investigator and needed some basic information on Lorene that I did not have.

Her name was Lorene Parker and I needed to find out her birthdate. I also knew that Jim Haggerty, the insurance agent in the building who shared offices with my dad, might help me. I took the chance and called. He was understanding. He and his wife were Mother's dearest and closest friends. They loved her and knew her well. He explained that Lorene had been hired by John almost twenty years ago and had come from a neighboring town looking for a job. As far as he was aware, she did not have any family in town but did have family in the city. I mentioned that there would be a private investigator nosing around soon for answers about Miss Lorene. He was supportive. "I understand, Claire. Let us know if there is anything we can do. You know how much we've always loved John and Nella. There may be nothing out of the ordinary here, but I can understand your concern and you have a right to find out."

The investigator took six weeks of snooping before his final report appeared in the mail. The large brown envelope lay on the table for two days staring at me. Finally, I got up enough nerve to open it. I began reading standing at the table then I lowered my quivering body into the closest chair. I felt weak and sick to my stomach. Lorene was raised in a small town about forty miles away. She went to high school there, but did not graduate. Her parents were deceased, and she had no children. So far, so good. Her credit was good, and she had no debts other than a car. She had rented a small house since coming to our town and had never purchased a home. I kept reading and scanning and hoping for something. But there was nothing out of the ordinary about Lorene that the investigator discovered. His remarks stated that he was not able to find out why she had not finished high school other than she dropped out in her senior year—the same year that I was born. How strange. I had to admit I was jumping to conclusions. What I needed was my actual birth certificate; I had a supplementary one issued when I was adopted which showed my adoptive parents, John and Nella Chastain. I called Michael knowing he would have a sensible suggestion.

"Claire, you are letting this thing get out of hand and eat away at you. It's got to stop. At some point, you will have to accept things at face value."

Minutes passed without a word. We could hear each other breathing. I bit my tongue to hold back hateful words I would regret. It would be unfair of me to expect Michael to know how I felt.

"Michael, you don't understand how difficult this is for me. My mother and dad were my world. Now some strange woman with ulterior motives has taken over my dad and his entire life. I might as well have never been born. I have become invisible and nonexistent in my dad's world, not to mention how my ill mother was treated. It's not right, and I won't stand for it."

I began crying hysterically.

"Claire, try to calm down. I'll be over in a few minutes, and we'll talk about it. Hang tight."

I hung up and sank to the chair. Maybe he was right. Maybe I was overdue for some much-needed introspection. Lorene might be the most evil-driven hag ever created and what would that prove? My dad was a grown man with all his mental faculties capable of making his own decisions. Yet I was not satisfied and accepting of reality.

Michael came through as always. He had his usual calming influence. Simply sitting with his arms around me on the sofa with my head on his shoulder, I felt comforted that all was not dark.

"Claire, I want to help you, but I think you have to consider realistically that you have a few options. You can try to accept Lorene and make the best of it, or you can continue to fight against her for no rational reason and make yourself miserable and not change anything."

Claire was listening politely.

"Michael, I want to petition the court for my adoption records."

"Why?"

"Because Lorene dropped out of high school the same year I was born. Don't you find that just too much of a coincidence?"

"Okay, now I have a question. What about asking your dad for the records?"

"Well, I thought about that but what if there is nothing to find out. Then I have upset him for no reason."

"Don't you think your dad deserves your trust? You are grown now, and he would understand you wanting to know about your birth parents."

I had overlooked one small detail. Unwittingly, I had transformed into a city slicker and had forgotten my country roots. How many private investigators does it take to attract attention in a small town? I got a phone call from Jim Haggerty saying that the investigator had not gone unnoticed. It was impossible for him to be subtle and clandestine—unpreventable because his precise presence screamed the warning

"Nosy stranger in town." No fault of his but that was enough to arouse suspicion. Luckily, he had done most of his snooping in the neighboring town, but there's still a grapevine between towns, trust me. I fully expected a call from my dad. And I got it.

"Claire, what in the world are you up to?" My dad did not sound happy. "What are you trying to prove? I know you've been checking on Lorene. So don't try to cover up."

I had to defend myself, but I hurriedly searched for a clever offensive position that took the edge off my selfish intentions.

"Well, I was concerned about you. Is that so terrible?"

I was still groping for an intelligent response from me.

"I hardly think you have any reason to be. If you wanted to know about her, you should have come to me. Going behind my back is not exactly the behavior I would expect from you, Claire. I am appalled. You are such a disappointment. This is something we should not discuss on the phone. I am coming up there tomorrow, so clear your calendar, Miss Pride of Podunk, Texas." His anger sent sparks through the telephone line.

Huh? He had never talked to me like that. *Our mutual respect had gone haywire and become vicious.* He was a trial lawyer on attack and not my dad. Then he hung up.

I wanted Michael to be there when my dad came but knew that would not set well. So when Dad rang the doorbell, I winced. I had to face the music. But then, dwarfed Claire took a deep breath, stood taller and straighter and became determined. My law training started to kick in. I automatically assumed the offense. I was not going to allow my own dad to push me around. I should be respectful, but I needed to hold my ground. I knew my rights. I had my family to protect.

"Claire, you had no right to go digging around for dirt on Lorene. She is my wife now, and you owe me respect even if you don't feel obliged to respect her." My inclination was right on. This confrontation was about to get ugly.

"Dad, I understand how you feel. I hope you will listen to what I have to say and can understand my point of view. This woman is a stranger to me. She maneuvered into position with you taking Mother's place before she had even taken her last breath. I don't appreciate Lorene's lack of respect for our family and particularly for my mother. Surely you can understand that; or, maybe not, since you don't seem to be bothered by what's become a circus sideshow. I also don't understand why you didn't confide in me. We have always been so close. But yet you chose to blindly charge ahead with Lorene taking over your life without any apparent feeling or concern for me."

John Chastain's eyes turned dark and his face flushed with anger. He was in no hurry, measuring every word.

"Claire, you have always been treated like a princess. You have gotten every material thing you ever wanted. Your mother and I loved you and catered to you as if you were the only child on earth. The last few years have tormented both of us. Now, you have your life ahead of you. I do not. I have a chance for happiness with someone I love. I am taking that chance while I can before I am so old and sick that no one wants me. I expected more from you. I had hoped that you would be happy for me and not act like some spoiled brat who has to have her way about everything. Who I marry is none of your business, and I do not need your permission. Lorene is a nice person, and she loves me. What else do you feel you need to know?"

I hesitated to play one of my aces in the hole. It was clear that my dad was intent on holding his position; that is, the investigator found nothing because there was nothing to find. I decided the moment was now. There would not be a good time for this discussion. It would never be an ideal occasion to confront or challenge John Chastain on anything—especially by me. For the first time, I challenged my father. I was, however, still questioning myself. Where did I get the strength and would I be sorry? I forged ahead. Foremost, I felt my father had betrayed our family and me.

"Dad, I know that Lorene dropped out of high school the year I was born."

All the color drained from my dad's face; he turned ashen gray. I was sorry the minute the sentence left my lips. Oh, my goodness, if I could retrieve my words! He did not have to give me a verbal response. His face and body language said it all. He contorted.

"Claire, you have crossed the line. There is nothing more to be said here."

We both took a moment.

"Sorry you feel that way, Dad. I just want what I am entitled to and, that is, to know the truth."

He turned toward her with tears in his eyes. "I was trying to protect you Claire. But that is no longer possible. You have succeeded in pushing me to the wall, so that I have no other option. Lorene is your birth mother."

I could hardly breathe. During basketball, I had the breath knocked out of me, but that was minor compared to the mac truck that had just hit and dragged me like a rag doll. My emotions had no substance to hang onto but were fractured in tiny pieces—like a bowl of stringy spaghetti. There was no substance or meaning to anything. Everything of substance in my world was *family*. Now there was not a shred of family for me to hold onto. I had dug and questioned and obsessed and now I had it out in the open—the ugly truth. Family meant nothing. The Chastain family was gone in the twinkling of an eye. All my cherished memories of my childhood and who I was as a person had been obliterated in those five words. There was no rational point of reference. My dad had married my birth mother! Is that perverted enough or is there more to this sordid tale that continues without end? Should I ask or be content with this A-bomb my own dad had just dropped. I was struggling to control my thoughts and emotions. I honestly felt a primitive urge to cry out like a wounded animal begging to be put out of its misery. I hated him in this moment and hated myself for ever loving him. I was drained dry devoid of feeling. Empty. I felt disdain and disgust. Who was this person now so unrecognizable that I wanted him out—out of my sight and out of my life.

We were both sobbing. I longed to be comforted by him, but that was impossible now. There was nothing that infiltrated our Chastain cocoon when my dad hugged me as a small and fragile child. The warmth of his love and affection enveloped me as an invisible shield from the contamination of the world. He was my protector always. Now the real John Chastain stood before me as a pitiful, vulnerable creature.

He was a stranger who chose to satisfy his own desires at any cost. Where is the John Chastain I knew or was he my grand concoction? Where was the man whose name was synonymous with integrity? Where was the man who loved Nella Claire Chastain so deeply that when he looked at her, they were the only two creatures on earth? Where was the father that I idolized and from childhood chose as the living model of whom I wanted to be? Where was the man so loved by his community because he stood for something that others merely aspired to? *All gone.* A lifetime with the vitality of hope running through my veins, now drained dry, leaving despair. He stood before me a stranger.

"Please leave now. You have nothing to say that will ever bring us back. No more hurt from you, please."

My dad looked a hundred years old. He arose from the sofa with his head down, feet plodding toward the door. I wanted to run to him. I needed him to know I still loved him. My pride, like a stalwart brick wall, surrounded me like a fortress. He had much more to say. But I wanted none of it. There was nothing he could say that I wanted to hear. I was numb.

He turned, "Claire, I know you are hurting, and I am sorry for that. I hope you will realize that I still love you. I should have told you sooner. Please forgive me." He closed the door.

I was left with nothing but my thoughts. After turning my world upside down and inside out, is that all you have to say to your daughter? How pitiful. You are a small, small man, John Chastain. My hero had fallen from Grace when I needed him the most.

Chapter 25. Levy & Chastain, LLP.

After the confrontation with my dad, I was a lost soul. I immediately called Michael. I needed his counsel, but mostly I needed him by my side. I had yet to tell him about the signed deed to Mother's property. I had to use my best maneuver to obtain the property and to outmaneuver my dad. When Michael opened the door, I ran to him and flung myself into his arms. I amazed myself how easily I let down my guard with him.

"It's a good thing you are here. This has been the most unbelievable day of my life."

She proceeded to describe the scene with her father finally owning up to the truth after she pushed him into a corner and pulled it out of him.

"You know, Michael, I would have been shocked when I learned about Lorene but having Dad deny up to the end made everything so much worse than it had to be. I'll never understand why he was so deceitful. Honesty from the beginning would have made the truth so much easier to swallow."

Michael said nothing for several minutes. He looked at her searching for some clue of what she expected him to say.

"Claire, at least it is all out in the open. I'm not sure there was any great time to learn about this. Your family has been in turmoil for years starting with your mother's illness. It's been one thing after another. I'm not defending him but at least try to see his position."

"I can't believe you're taking his side. Why can't you see *my* position? You have no idea what it means to have your family turned upside down. It's not that easy to just forgive and forget everything that's dumped on you, then skip arm in arm down the yellow brick road."

"Claire, that's not fair. I'm not taking his side against you. I know you're hurting. I don't want this contention between us. It's your personal decision, and I admit, you're right, I've not been through what you are going through."

He didn't have to look at Claire; he knew her well enough to know she was puffed up and pouting.

"You do have to decide where you and I go from here—at least professionally. We have our future to think about. Do you still want to open our law practice?"

"Good grief yes. If there is anything that I am 100% sure about, it's our partnership. There is something else that I need to tell you. Mother signed a warranty deed transferring her home place to me. Dad does not know. How in the world am I going to do this? I want that land and it's my right to have it. We have to figure out how to make that happen."

We talked into the night over several glasses of wine. I'm not sure how much good the talking did, but the wine worked great; at least it served as a temporary pacifier. Michael still clung to his tired old idea of my going to my dad to work the matter out between us. I, on the other hand, was inclined to record the deed and let the chips fall where they may. I was annoyed by just the thought that it might be necessary to have any dealings with my dad.

"He is going to fight you every inch of the way if you record that deed without telling him. Hear me on this one, Claire; it's one bad idea. You two will end up in a legal battle. Think about what all that involves. Do you want all that stress when we are just beginning our law practice? Do you want Chastain v. Chastain to be our first case?"

We agreed that I should sleep on it and that it was past time to put this sorry day to bed.

The next day Michael had several appointments scheduled for us to look at office space which was a welcome distraction from the Chastain fiasco. The first office we saw was about the right square footage, but the location was lousy. The second space had a good location but was small, and we had to share space with another lawyer down the hall. The third space had a great location near the courthouse but was way over our budget. His parents were pretty much footing the tab for our start-up, so we needed to stay the course and not overspend. We almost talked ourselves into leasing the last space; it would save time and therefore money being so close to the courthouse. I wanted to see all our options before deciding. Michael mentioned that he had heard about an area on the edge of downtown being renovated. There was a small house that had been converted to office space in an up-and-coming part of town, and the rent was affordable.

Several other businesses had already located there—an independent insurance agency, a small restaurant, and several retail shops. It was fifteen minutes from my apartment on the edge of downtown and accessible to the courthouse. The rent was comparable to the other places we had seen. It had a reception area and four small offices served by a kitchen and bathroom. The gleaming old pine hardwood floors had recently been refinished, and the place had been freshly painted. One office had built-in bookshelves on every wall crying out for a law library. The eye-catcher for me was the front covered porch with an ideal spot for our "Levy & Chastain" shingle. We signed the lease.

Michael had passed the Bar exam on his first try. I did not. I had to re-take the exam in a few months. In the meantime, we had gotten a few clients by referral through his parents. We were excited about our new venture. His parents had been wonderful and supportive and even enthusiastic about our legal partnership. We agreed that our personal lives should be put on hold. Our first priority was our law practice. I was sure his parents had no small part in our decision. I was good enough to be his law partner, but it was questionable whether I was acceptable as his life partner. I was ecstatic that they accepted me on any level—for now. It crossed my mind that we might be one of those couples who are together for life but never marry. Time would tell. I conceded that the religion thing would not go away and the partnership that made sense now for Michael and me was practicing law. I was fully aware of my label: *Shiksa.*

The next few months were all about the details of getting the space ready, business cards and stationery, phones, office equipment, hiring a secretary. The first thing we did was order our sign. The wooden block rectangle said it to the world. We are ready and able to be your legal representatives: Levy & Chastain, LLP. Being so busy was a welcome diversion from my problems, and unbelievably I hadn't thought much about my dad and Lorene. Perhaps I was self-centered, but I wanted to focus on my future, not on my past. I wanted to think about pleasant and positive and new beginnings, not about dark and negative and problems with no solutions.

My mindset about Lorene had not changed. I did not have the slightest interest in getting to know her or having a relationship with her. I was grateful she carried me full term and that she had the foresight to give me up for adoption to such deserving, loving parents. I was grateful, but I refused to be indebted. Quite simply, I did not like her, did not want her as my surrogate mother, and could not respect her. There was no going back to fix this. She put her claws into my dad early on with my mother alive and knowing full well what she was doing. Furthermore, she isolated my dad from me deliberately driving a huge wedge between us. Her behavior was cruel, self-serving and unforgivable. I saw through her scheme. I clung to my hope that my dad would see through her and come to his senses.

Meanwhile, I intended to get on with my life. Nothing and no one was going to get in my way. I thought about my childhood dream of being a lawyer with my dad. That dream could have been real except it was my dream, not my dad's. I longed to have him in the beginning of my career and a part of my and Michael's lives. Dad would always be my mentor. In spite of all the trouble between us, my dad remained my role model. I should call him and clear the tension between us. How many chances does a daughter have to share a moment so important? It has been two months since our blow-up, or it might be our break-up. Honestly, Claire, how can you break up with your father? I had no idea how that could work and deep down I did not want to find out. For sure, I would have to make the first move. The various scenarios danced in my head. Dad, I want to have a relationship with you but not with your wife. Dad, I want you back in my life if you dump what's-her-face. How ridiculous to consider calling him. He would think I had changed my position: that I was willing to forgive and forget; that I wanted warm and fuzzy with him and Lorene. Not going to happen.

My biological connection to Lorene was not severed with the cutting of the umbilical cord. I admit that. But the emotional ties were severed when she gave me up for adoption and cannot be re-connected. Her recent actions have reinforced my opinion. She is the epitome of shallow and selfish. She is a user and offensive. I will never understand why my father refuses to see her true colors. How many times can this go around and around and over and over in my brain? It changes nothing, and I have to let go of it. Thankfully, I was rescued by the ringing of the phone.

Chapter 26. Crisis in Costa Rica

Angela Callaghan was calling. She was flying to Costa Rica. Libby was sick in a hospital in San José. Bam. Bam. Bam. I was numb. No, no—I refused to believe this was happening.

"I have to go to her. When are you leaving?"

"I was about to make my airline reservations this morning and was hoping that you could go with me. There's a flight leaving tonight at 10:30, and there are a few seats left. Evan had planned to go, but he cannot leave the Ranch right now. Also, I may be there indefinitely. I plan to bring Libby home once she is well enough to travel. We don't know when that might be."

"Angela, thank goodness you called me. I'll meet you at the gate."

My mind twirled as I glanced at my watch—9:30. I have to call Michael, pack, find my passport and get to the airport twenty minutes away. I should have plenty of time if I could just calm down. I had to think. Pack light and take warm weather clothes. I dreaded calling Michael. He must think I am one walking trauma after another. But my dread was uncalled for. He was concerned and understanding and calming. He assured me there was no need to hurry and that he would take me to the airport. I told him I felt guilty leaving him with a new, struggling law practice but the bad timing could not be helped.

"Claire, don't worry about anything here. I can handle it. I know some people from law school who can help me out if necessary. The most important thing is Libby now. I'll be home by five, so we don't have to rush to get you on the plane. We can have a quiet dinner before you go."

Once at the airport, we said our good-byes at the curb outside the gate. Tears were pooling up.

"Claire, try to take this as it comes. Wait and see how Libby is before you load yourself down with worry. I know you have every reason to be concerned, but Libby and Angela need you now. Remember, I can be there if you need me. Take care, my love."

At the gate, I spotted Angela pacing nervously. She ran towards me and hugged me gently. I could feel her relief.

"Oh, Claire. It means so much to have you with me. You'll never know how much Evan and I appreciate it. I know this is a shock, but everything happened so quickly. Since we have several minutes before boarding, I'll fill you in with what I know. We got the last seats on this flight, and they're not together so let's go to the coffee shop after we check in."

Angela began to speak slowly wiping away the tears. Libby got ill about three weeks ago with what they thought was the flu. Her fever had continued to climb and had stayed in the 102-103° range for the last week. She had been quarantined as a precaution since the doctors hadn't diagnosed the problem and didn't know if she was contagious. She had undergone a spinal tap and bone marrow test which were both inconclusive. Leukemia was suspected or some type of fever such as typhoid or malaria. It had been difficult to understand the doctor over the phone, so she had limited information. She was in the dark almost as much as I about Libby's condition. We had to wait and pray.

"Claire, there is something I have wanted to tell you for years. You have been a Godsend to our family especially to Libby. We all know it was because of you that she was able to cope with the tremendous change of losing her family and becoming a member of our family. We are eternally grateful and love you for all you have done. Even though we talked about this before, I must tell you again how much you have meant to our family."

"I appreciate that Angela, but no thanks are necessary. You and Evan have been so good for Libby and have brought her more happiness than she has ever known. I do love Libby like a sister, and it all came naturally for us. She and I have discussed this so often that our lives were destined to connect. We have completed each other's lives, and she has completed our family."

"Claire, there's one other thing. While I was putting away some of

Libby's things when she left for Costa Rica, I found a red spiral notebook of hers. She apparently wrote it during the split up of her family. It is the most endearing, heartfelt message I have ever read. I think you will agree. I think she will forgive us this one time for snooping. She left it in the drawer of her bedside table. I realize now that I should have done more to help her get through it all. I was too distant, but I have to admit I wasn't sure what to do."

I took the tattered pages and put it in my briefcase as we boarded the plane and got settled in for the long flight. I was apprehensive about reading Libby's private thoughts, but I trusted Angela. She wouldn't ask me to do anything that would hurt Libby or me.

I was at the back of the plane and saw Angela several rows ahead of me. She was exhausted, and I hoped she could get some rest. I reached into my briefcase and pulled out the red notebook which was written so long ago that the penciled writing had faded until it was barely legible.

I hoped that she would forgive me for the intrusion. Could anyone be more intimate? I doubt it. Although I believed I knew Libby as well as one human can know another, as I began reading, I confessed I was entering another world—the unknown sacred abyss of another's soul.

Who are the DeLaneys?

They are my family. My mother is Ella. I am Libby (Elizabeth), age 10. My little brothers are Aaron, 6; Jacob, 4; Christopher, 3; and my little sister Hannah is 2. We are what most people call needy. That would be our category. We have pride in spite of being poor and being dependent on other people sometimes. Our mother teaches us to take care of what we do have and to be thankful.

My brothers and I love to play outdoors, climb trees and watch the trains go by. We are not supposed to play on the tracks, but sometimes we can't help it. My little sister is our love. She is the cutest baby girl in the world. I carry her a lot just so I can hug her and kiss her. I take care of her and make sure she takes her bottle, and I change her diapers. She gets so mad her little round face turns red as a tomato, and she kicks and throws a hissy fit. She gets mad because she can't go with us when we leave the house to run around.

My brothers are so good and mind me. They know I am a big sis and do what I say so they won't get hurt. We don't have toys, but we have fun.

When we moved to this town, Dalton DeLaney, who was our Daddy, had been killed in a construction accident last year and my mother had been taking care of us by herself without any help for the last year. When we move to a town, Mother makes sure that I go to school and the teachers always help us every way they can. In the last town, my fifth-grade teacher told the Baptist Church we needed help, so they brought us food and clothes. Mother didn't want to ask for help, but she had to until the insurance check came from the construction company. We have been living on that money, but it has run out. Now our family is in big trouble. We don't have any family to turn to. But now we have met a good friend.

We moved to this town May 26, 1955. A very nice man named John saw us on the road looking for coke bottles to take to the store to sell to make money. He stopped his truck and told us to be careful. Then he brought his daughter Claire and her mother with food and clothes for us. I ran out the back door because I don't want strangers to see us in trouble. But I know my little brothers and sister have to have milk and food from someplace. I think God sent this man to help us.

I wanted to get a job to help my family, but no one wants to hire me and pay me any money because I am too young and too little. If we could just get by for a little longer, it won't be long before I can help Mother get groceries and take care of all of us. It is too much for her to feed and clothe and get everything else that children need.

This friend is someone special and cares about us. In most places we lived, people ran away from us and didn't want their kids to have anything to do with us. But this man wanted his daughter to be our friend. I guess because we are different most people are scared of us, but there is no reason. We are clean, and our mother teaches us to be good people. She will not stand for us to be bad. She says we may be poor, but we have pride and respect and know how to treat other people. She says it is simple. We treat other people like we want to be treated—kind. That is from the Bible. I learned that from my mother and in Sunday School. She also said something about don't be so quick to judge other people. You haven't walked in their shoes.

Claire and I are the same age and in the same grade. She is my best friend and loves me no matter what I am. She is the first person I ever knew like that. She brings light to my life. I am afraid of what the future holds. I try to remember that I will have Claire and her family to help me.

Mother is tired now and afraid for her children. She has to have a solution for our family. She will give us all away to different families all over the country. These are people that John Chastain found for us. I will be the first to go out the door, and I won't come back. I did not tell my little ones that. I told Mother not to come out on the ugly porch to wave and say good-bye like the little ones did. She didn't.

I promised Mother I'd be a good girl and bring happiness and no trouble to the Callaghans. They live on a big ranch, and I don't know them. They are strangers, but they still want to adopt me. All my little ones have good homes, too.

I asked God to send someone to help us, and now he did so it is up to me. Mother said we all have to make adjustments in life and that some will be hard and some even harder. She is smart, and I believe what she tells me. She must have a broken heart. She had to give away all her precious children. But I know she loves me that much and all the little ones, too. So that means I have to make the best of it. She is the one who made the big sacrifice for us. I worry now about who will take care of her. She depended on me.

So that is my story of the DeLaneys. We are not a family together anymore, but I feel like we will always be a family deep in my heart. Because a family is forever.

Libby
10/28/55

Chapter 27. Turning Point

As I closed the tattered pages, I became a bewildered child again. I could not stop the tears. I was consumed with a sadness that overtook my being that I had not felt since Libby and I were children. The memories of our childhood as our lives intersected and our souls connected filled me with humbleness and thankfulness. How was it that I had been so blessed to have her in my life? She had been through so much heartache and emotional adjustment. But she refused to hang onto the past and rose above it all. Once branded a misfit from the other side of the tracks, she set her sights on becoming the type of person she envisioned and not what other people labeled her. The painful past did not have to be read to be re-lived. There was no need for a written reminder except for this tribute—Libby's tribute to her family but also a tribute to her. Our journey together began when we were just kids. We didn't hold back. We were simply two kids who, when we looked into each other's eyes, all we saw was complete and utter trust. We felt no threat and no need to hold back. So we didn't. And to this day we see the same reflection of trust. And the reward has been glorious.

I looked anxiously toward the front of the plane. Angela must not see how upset I am. I powdered my nose, applied fresh lipstick and some cologne and made myself feel better. My spirits lifted when we arrived at the sleek, modern hospital. I had not been sure what to expect and was reassured by what I saw. The head nurse explained that they still had not diagnosed the cause of Libby's fever. As a precaution, we were asked to wear masks and gloves when entering her room. Libby had been critically ill two nights ago with fever that soared to 105°. They kept her packed in ice throughout the night to try to bring down her fever. She was weak, but resting, and her temperature had gradually lowered to 102°. I looked through the glass and saw my precious friend.

I felt myself start to crumble. I took Angela's hand as we approached Libby's bed.

"Libby, sweetheart, it's mom Angela and Claire. Can you hear us?"

Libby's voice was weak, but clear. Her blue eyes were cloudy and her face flushed. "Hi, Mom. Oh Claire, thank goodness you're here. I am so glad to see you. I dreamed you came."

Angela came nearer Libby's bedside, "It is not a dream now, honey. We are here, and we'll be with you as long as you need us."

She reached out for us. Immediately I saw how thin her once slender arms were. I was shocked she had lost so much weight. We squeezed her hand and then she closed her eyes. She was relieved that we were there but she was exhausted. We should come back later.

The doctor met us in the hallway and introduced himself as Dr. Pasqual, her doctor and the head of the hospital. He ushered us into a small conference room and gave us a summary of her symptoms and treatment. They had treated her fever and had given her antibiotics. Results of her tests did not show any definitive illness, although it was obvious she had an infection. They were targeting her elevated white blood cell count and watching it for some change or pattern. Two nights before we arrived had been significant. He was reluctant to put too much emphasis on the extraordinary high fever, but he felt it was a sign that her fever broke since it gradually declined since the crisis.

He looked intently at us as he continued, "She is a sick girl. We are severely limited in treatment because we have not diagnosed the illness. We can treat her with broad spectrum medications which may or may not be effective. We have to be persevering and patient. This may well be a fever of unknown origin which is not uncommon."

Angela began to cry. I put my arms around her and whispered. "We know our girl. She is strong and determined. She is getting the best medical care. She can get well."

The doctor continued, "I have to tell you that, during her preliminary examination, I noted that she has a heart condition, a murmur caused by a faulty heart valve. I wondered if you were aware and if it had caused her any symptoms or problems."

Angela's eyes flashed knowingly, "Why, yes. We adopted Libby when she was ten, almost eleven years old, and took her to the doctor for a checkup. Our family doctor told us she seemed healthy but that she did have a heart murmur. He felt that, unless it caused her any problems, there was no need for additional treatment. We told Libby but did not make a big deal out of it. We didn't want to frighten her. She assured us she felt fine and, if she noticed anything unusual in the way she felt, she would let us know."

Dr. Pasqual nodded. "That is a concern I have with this high fever continuing for so long, and I will continue to monitor her closely as the next forty-eight hours are critical. Based on my experience with fevers of this kind, I think she passed the critical stage two nights ago, but let's be cautious until we know. But for now, I think we have every reason to be optimistic that she is recovering."

The doctor saw our relief and our exhaustion. "Please. Feel free to relax here for a few minutes. I know you have traveled all night. There is a nice hotel, although small, a few blocks away. If you want, I can have someone call and get you a room. I'll get all the information for you."

Angela and I thanked him. When he closed the door, we held each other, sobbing uncontrollably. We were relieved, worried, thankful, apprehensive, confused— name an emotion—but mostly we were thankful for Libby, for her good medical care and for having each other to see us through this.

The next day Libby's temperature had dropped to the 101-100° range. She was eating and strong enough to sit and make short trips down the hallway. Angela and I were amazed how much she had improved. The doctor was still cautious, but he was pleased with her progress. Over the next week, her temperature continued to decline, and Libby became stronger. Once it reached 99°, the doctor suggested that he might consider letting her leave the hospital to stay in the hotel with us for a week. If she did well, then he would release her to travel.

We three were as giddy as kids. We had Libby back! Her appetite was voracious; she hardly finished a meal before she was planning what she wanted to eat next. She had gained a few pounds and was ready to go home.

Angela had brought up the subject somewhat sheepishly. She wasn't sure how Libby felt about going home. We thought she should return home but what did Libby think? Angela wanted her to make the decision but hoped it was the one to return home.

"I'm ready to come home. I have learned so much, and there is much to be done here. But in a way, I was running from my problems. I feel prepared to teach now and to share my experience. I hope there is a place for me at my old school. I know deep in my heart that's where I belong."

We spent another two weeks in San José and then we were on our way back home. It had been a long, mysterious illness and recovery. After monitoring her white cell count all these weeks, Dr. Pasqual still had not been able to definitively diagnose her illness. By the time she sought treatment, she had been so run down and her immune system so compromised that the infection was severe and life-threatening. He confided to Angela that he had treated one other patient this severely stricken with similar symptoms, and that patient died. He instructed Angela and Libby that she was to see her doctor as soon as she got back home. He also felt she should have further cardiac testing as a precaution due to her heart murmur and the prolonged fever. He also prescribed rest, rest, and plenty of good food. She needed to get back to her normal weight.

Angela and I were talking like magpies, so excited that we didn't rest on the plane. We commented on how great Libby looked and what a fighter she was. I flashed back to our night flight to Costa Rica. What a difference these few weeks have made. We were grateful to have her coming home, yet proud of her for what she had accomplished. I glanced over at Libby sleeping peacefully in the airline seat, partially reclined, but still curled up in the form of a human pretzel. She was not waiting for the luxury of sleeping in her own bed. Those were four long years. I hoped we would never be separated again. It was time to make up for lost time. Libby's prayers had been answered: *Divine gift of renewal of the spirit.*

Chapter 28. Chastain v Chastain

No matter how boring and mundane we feel life gets, it is comforting to know the world we wake up in each day. Libby was back at the Ranch with the Callaghans. She was anxious to get to work, but was under Angela's watchful eye, which meant she had to follow doctor's orders. She had applied at the local school to teach middle school or high school English in the fall. It was her dream to come back to teach at her old school, and she had to do her best to make it a reality. But for now, she was content to be on the ranch she loved, recuperating and getting back to her old self. She realized that she was not as strong physically as she hoped.

I was in the office working with Michael trying to catch up. I was astounded. In the weeks I had been away, we had twenty new active cases. Michael had been busy. He was working on a trust agreement and several wills that I hoped I would help him draft. He also had to draft some real estate and employment contracts. But most exciting to me were a couple of family law cases which I hoped to take over. I would *retake* the bar exam again soon, then I would work cases on my own without needing him to sign off my pleadings with his bar number. Things were progressing. While I was away, I had plenty of time to think about the future. I was convinced I wanted to specialize in family law. I guess you have to hit some people in the face to get their attention. Why had it taken me so long to realize that was the path for me? I yearned to find meaning and satisfaction in the practice of law and understood that helping families going through troubled times was the answer.

"Michael, I had a chance to do a lot of thinking in Costa Rica. I want to practice family law. I've seen firsthand the heartbreak of broken families. We can make a good practice with all the divorce and broken homes. It may not be as lucrative, but I know it is right for me."

"Good for you, Claire. It sounds like you have been busy, too. We may have to take whatever cases we can get for a while, but I know we can build a family law practice. You certainly have the temperament for it with some patience. We can build our reputation and the type of practice we want. So yes, you'll do most of the family law, and I'll handle the business law and contracts. How does that sound?"

"Great then. We're in agreement. I hope you agree with something else I've decided to do. I've decided to push to get the land. I should telephone Dad. He needs to know that I have the Warranty Deed signed by Mother before I record it with the county clerk. I've delayed this whole mess long enough."

"Claire, just some friendly advice. Think again about this deed thing. It's foolhardy to think he's going to be okay with it. Try to patch things up with him. You and he need each other, and you're family, and we need him in our lives."

What he said was true, but it was more complicated. I hated it when Michael was right, and he was making a habit of that lately. But I knew what I wanted and what I had to do to get it.

I glanced at my watch—four o'clock—a good time to call. Please don't let Lorene answer. I did not feel equipped to deal with that. Dad answered on the second ring. "Hi, Dad. How are you doing? It's your wayward daughter home from Costa Rica."

"Hi, Claire. It's good to hear your voice and glad you're back. Michael called and said you had gone with Angela—that Libby was pretty sick— and y'all were bringing her home."

He sounded somewhat receptive although cool. After all, we had not spoken since our emotional impasse a few months ago.

"Yes, she's back home at the Ranch. She was extremely ill, but she's on the mend now, and I am so glad to have her back. She and I do not do well separated."

"Dad, I know you and I are going through a rough patch, and I don't like it. Shouldn't we try to resolve our differences? I want us to try to work things out. I realize that some things are the way they are and can't be changed. We will just have to live with it. But there's been something hanging over my head that I need to clear up. I hope you will understand."

"Claire, I'm happy to hear you have come to your senses. I must say I'm at a loss as to how to talk to you lately. So it will be a relief to have an intelligent conversation."

"Dad, before Mother died, she insisted that I draw up a Warranty Deed transferring title to her home place to me. I've kept that deed she signed not sure what to do. I wanted you to know. She knew how special that land is to me. I was uncomfortable with the whole idea, but she told me she could not rest easy until she had done her best to see that her wishes were carried out. I didn't want to proceed with recording the deed until I talked to you."

Silence. Seconds might as well have been eons.

"Dad, are you there?"

"Claire, how dare you. I am again amazed at your brazen tactics. You will go to any lengths to get what you want without regard for anyone else."

"Dad, don't be so darn pig-headed and unreasonable. I'm trying here to confide in you, but you are making it exceedingly difficult. You know she wanted me to have it. We all talked about how the property belonged in the family and that we would do everything in our power to see that no outsider got the land. The way you are acting is exactly why I didn't tell you earlier."

"No. Don't try that with me. Here is the way this played out, my devious, manipulating, calculating daughter. You saw an opportunity and capitalized on it. Nella was sick and weak and you took advantage of your own mother. I won't stand for your conniving. We did not raise a daughter who plots against her family who is utterly devoid of loyalty to her parents. You are so blinded by your desires and what you want that you used your own dying mother for your personal gain. I say you'll get this property when Hell freezes over and not one second before."

"But Dad—" Click. The line was dead, and I was numb. But more than anything, I was furious that I had allowed myself to be attacked so viciously by my own father. What I wanted to say was: I will get this land come Hell or high water! I was just as mean and nasty as my dad. I started to cry. Listen to yourself, Claire. What glory was there in that?

What had happened to us?

The voice belonged to my father, but I did not believe the words were coming from his lips. What in the world has happened to John Chastain? He continued to reinforce my disappointment and my disbelief. What did I expect? On second thought, I would have been shocked if he had reacted any differently. Deep within, he would not be accepting of the idea if, for no other reason, that foremost he is a lawyer. In the legal world especially, sick people making last-minute property bequests don't set well—either within or outside the family.

What was clear: if I hoped to get this land, I had to fight for it. I was surprised at my own resolve. There had been a period that I would have never gone against my father about anything. Now the fierceness of my determination to defeat him frightened me.

Although he was empathetic, Michael offered no support for my cause. He admittedly did not understand my obsession with Mother's land. He absolutely would not support my dispute with my father. Family meant everything to him, and it was impossible for him to understand the choice I appeared to be making and the door I was willing to close.

"He is your family, Claire. You should back down on this. It's not worth the sacrifice. You could lose your dad forever. You have already crossed the line with him. Come on, you'll get the land someday anyway. Be the bigger person and reach out to him. Trust me. You will regret pursuing this ugliness."

His words fell on my deaf ears. I didn't need his approval although I could have used his support. But I had to recognize the differences between Michael and me. I was raised in the country in a state where land especially family land means everything. You do whatever is necessary to hold on to it and to keep it in the family. He saw me as sacrificing family for a piece of land. I didn't know how to impress upon him the difference and to express how we cherished the land. Maybe you had to feel it. Merely telling someone was a feeble, futile effort. Feelings run deep when land was part of the family for generations.

"Michael, do you believe what you are saying? I doubt it. The gold-digging, money-grubbing new Mrs. Chastain will see to it that I do not get Mother's home place, **ever!** That is a given. What nonsense to believe otherwise."

I decided to record the deed in the county clerk's office Monday morning. If I needed an affidavit, I knew who to go to. I mulled all night plotting my strategy and how to bring my father to his knees.

The next day, I called Mother's dearest friend, Jim Haggerty. He had been a big help when I hired the detective to check out Lorene. He and his wife Millie would help me. Logically, I was putting him on the spot, but emotionally I counted on his and Millie's loyalty to Mother.

"Jim, I need your help. I wouldn't bother you, but you and Millie were Mother's best friends. There is no one else I can turn to."

In the midst of my explanation of what was happening between Dad and me, Jim unexpectedly interrupted. "Claire, I already know. Your dad came over to see Millie and me last night. I don't think I've ever seen him this upset. He was on the verge of collapse. I am genuinely worried about him."

"Well, he has me upset too. Mother wanted me to have the land. Period. End of story. If he loved and cared about me and respected Mother, he would do everything in his power to see that happened, instead of acting like a jackass. Heaven knows, he owes her and me at least that much. Besides, it was her land, not his. She inherited it from her parents. He was never out one dime. Mother even paid the taxes. I can't tell you how often she said, "I know Claire loves this land as much as I do. Someday it will belong to her."

"Claire, I know you are still upset about your dad and Lorene. But you are piling on more bad feelings than your relationship can handle. I seriously wonder if you realize what you are asking of him. Let me talk to him and see if this can be worked out privately."

"Fine. But Monday morning I am recording the deed."

"Okay, Claire. It's your decision. But you need to know he is prepared to fight you with everything he's got. He has mentioned coercion by you, so that Nella under duress signed over the deed to you. It's food for thought as to how bad this can get, and it's still in the beginning stages. I'll do what I can."

"Thanks, Jim, for the warning, but I am not intimidated by John

Chastain and his high-handed tactics."

Michael and I did not have a good weekend. He was sullen and swelled up like a bullfrog. I was my usual prideful, full-speed-ahead, with-blinders-on, self.

Jim called me early Monday morning before the courthouse opened. He made it clear that he was acting as mediator and therefore he had no favorites. A meeting between Jim, my dad and me was scheduled for that Wednesday. He also encouraged us to think about our bargaining positions and to weigh the consequences using worst-case scenario in assessing the outcome of our actions. Also, what compromise(s) if any were each of us willing to make?

"Soul-searching time, Claire, for you both. Are you willing to sever your relationship with your dad forever? And I have to say this so you'll pardon me if I step over the line. I wonder: how proud of yourself will you be when this whole thing is over?"

Over the next two days, my brain whirled with questions that I did not want to answer. I wrestled day and night with my conscience and my ego fighting for position. What was my objective and why? Was the cost worth it? Was I acting irrationally? Was I lashing out at my father because I was hurt and disappointed in him and still seething from his behavior during Mother's last days? Would I regret dragging my dad and me through the mud? What about the legal ramifications such as affidavits, probate court inquiries, appearances and depositions? What about the public humiliation?

I drove to the meeting bleary-eyed and exhausted. I tried to get my thoughts together in a brain that was on overload and sleep-deprived. I was grateful and relieved that Jim had stepped in the middle of our dispute. I realized how rare a friend he (and Millie) was to our family that he cared enough about us to get involved in this mess. For certain, he did not need our aggravation. He loved us both, so I'm sure he was agonizing as well. I was not anxious to make the Chastains front page news even in the Gazette. And then there was my startling revelation— I questioned my motives.

We met in Jim's office conference room. It was small, comfortable and familiar. The coffee smelled good, and Millie was at the front desk smiling and gracious. She had worked in the office with Jim for as long as I could remember. Just like John and Nella, they worked side by side.

"Hi Claire sweetheart. It's wonderful to see you. We miss seeing your beautiful face. Would you care for a soft drink or something besides coffee?"

"Hi Millie. I'm fine with coffee." I hugged her. She reminded me of Mother with her same sweet, polite and soothing demeanor. She and Mother were of the same era. Self-controlled and disciplined and always courteous no matter the circumstances. I was thankful—Lorene was nowhere to be seen.

Dad had not arrived. Jim took me into the conference room to settle in and then he turned and left the room leaving me alone with my thoughts. Over and over in my head, the same old tired phrase repeated. "Remember, Claire, just because you have to compromise doesn't mean you give up."

At precisely 10:00, I heard my dad's voice and the butterflies took over my stomach, I was in first grade again. My dad entered the room, and I arose from my chair. We greeted each other with a brief handshake and half-hearted hug—adversaries but courteous. I was struggling to hold back the tears. How could this be happening?

Jim began the meeting with some brief comments. He handed us a paper to complete which was an outline of what each of us expected and what each of us was willing to contribute to resolve this issue. I suddenly felt ridiculous and humiliated. Isn't this first-year law school mediation mock court stuff? And to think I was one of the parties—a perfect example of how nice people wind up in the courts to solve their problems. There are legitimate legal issues which must be settled in a court of law. But there are also cases where underlying personal issues take over and present as legal dilemmas. It's making a sideshow of your family affairs. Court should be the last resort.

I looked up from my mediation paper and saw my dad. I was startled and shaken by what I saw. Every line and wrinkle showed as a deep crevice. His once bright blue eyes were red-rimmed and blurry. These were signs of the ravages of time and gravity for sure but also accentuated by the emotional stress that I helped impose. I hated myself. Before I could restrain, I reached across the table for his hand and briefly touched the perfectly-ironed and stiffly-starched cuff of his white shirt. I smelled the clean, fresh scent that was always my father. In spite of it all, he was still my father, and I loved him beyond my wildest imaginings. I was hurt and disappointed and estranged from him, but I could not live with myself unless I did my part to remedy all that. I had to let go of my anger and forgive him.

Jim left the room. Dad and I waited in silence for the first one to speak.Dad began. "Claire, you must remember always that you are my beloved daughter. No one and nothing will ever change that. I want us to work this out without any further heartache."

I felt the hot tears welling up. I must not cry and appear pitiful and out of control.

"Dad, me too. I admit that I have been hurtful. It's just that I wonder if you have forgotten me and what our family means to each other."

"There is not a day that goes by that I don't think of Nella. We both are still coping with losing her, but we have to go on without her. You and I are trying to build new lives, but we are still father and daughter. It will take mutual adjustment, but we can have our new lives and still be family."

"I want that more than anything, Dad."

"I'm willing to do my part to make that happen, Claire."

"Me, too. I'm sorry."

I ran to hug him and to tell him how much I loved him. The meeting was over. There was no further discussion about the home place or deeds or Lorene. This was neither the time nor the place. We needed healing and recovery and to trust each other again. Our fragile relationship was like a newborn fawn struggling to stand. It would take time to heal the wounds and make us strong again. I realized that a large portion of my parents' legacy to me was more than a piece of land. It was love of family. Not just in the smooth and easy times but in the rough and upside-down times. I did not need to defeat my father to hold my head high; in fact, the opposite was true. I could hold my head high, because I loved and respected my dad. Even in my hurt and insecurity, I hoped we could rebuild and be the Chastain father and daughter again. This was the right decision. I had to give up this land and with it my mother's dream and mine. Maybe I was entitled to the land, but at what cost. I refused to believe I was giving up and settling. That was the devil pulling my strings. I refused to sacrifice my father for 865 acres. I had confronted my own demon of selfishness and recognized the crucial consequences. *One of life's dreaded no do-over decisions. Family.*

Chapter 29. Our Broadway Star

I needed diversion and time away. I was emotionally drained and exhausted. Libby and I needed time together, and we grabbed our chance. We flew to New York over a long weekend to see Joanna. We were celebrating—I had passed the Bar and proudly added the elusive new number to my arsenal of personal identification. And Libby was feeling great. I was recognized by the State of Texas as an attorney and licensed to practice. That was heady stuff—I was enjoying my achievement at last. It was the first time in a long time that I felt I had something to celebrate.

It was Libby's first visit to the Big Apple, and we crammed every minute full of seeing the sights. Joanna acted as tour guide and made sure we checked off as many tourist have-to-sees as we could—Statue of Liberty, Empire State Building, Staten Island, and the Museum of Modern Art, short stroll through Central Park and dinner at Tavern on the Green. Joanna had not changed; she had one tempo—throttle wide open. Tonight she was our main attraction and topped off our visit as the cherry on top. We had followed Joanna's journey to its culmination on Broadway (no big surprise), but we couldn't believe we were here to see it!

After two years at the university with the Strutters (the last one as captain), Joanna was ready for a change. She wrote me occasionally, and I read her letters again and again to make sure I did not miss one iota. She returned to California, but was restless. She relocated to New York and studied acting with the best acting coaches and had taken singing and dancing lessons. She was endlessly working to improve her craft and auditioning for every role imaginable. "It's just part of it," she assured me, "you have to believe that you will get the next role." But she sounded tired. I wasn't sure if she was trying to convince herself or me.

She had once longed to be a Rockette but cautioned me not to expect too much too soon. She described the competition as fierce and dismissed her fellow female competitors in a few other not-to-be-repeated descriptive terms.

She landed two off-Broadway shows in the next two years, and I was in New York to see her in both productions. She assured me that she would get the lead in the next play and that it will come before our white hair and rocking chairs.

She is doing what she loves in the city she loves. "I am living my dream," she assured me, her eyes shining. I feel invigorated and relieved for her that she wasn't disappointed in her dreams. It gave me hope for my own dreams. I thought of the countless new stories to be told and discovered, plays to be written and movies to be made. If I didn't learn anything else from Joanna, I learned that we all have the right (and responsibility) to create. The celebrity stage is the venue for a select few. It may take a lifetime, but we have to pursue our dreams to find our own "stage" to showcase our talent. Her words resonated, "I know it's hard, Claire, but try not to continually compare yourself to others. It doesn't do any good. Mostly, we become either self-inflated or depressed."

Ten years after she left us, Libby and I were sitting orchestra center at the Impresario Theater on Broadway. Joanna needs no spotlight. Shining in the bright lights center stage, Joanna is singing and dancing her heart out. This sophisticated New York audience seems captivated. I am not surprised. I look at Libby. She hasn't taken her eyes off Joanna for the entire evening. I take a deep breath and smile smugly to myself—even a country bumpkin like me knows Star Quality. In a way, we are on that stage with you. Our lives touched and we are forever intertwined. So take a bow for us, Joanna. Once again, you are not a stranger in town.

We went backstage to congratulate her, and she looked amazing as always. I hugged her and told her I always knew she was going to be a star. She asked about my dad with eyes wide awaiting my answer. I briefly explained he had remarried. She was not surprised. Then she continued to say in a strict tone that he was a man who shouldn't be alone. She continued to say that he must have been lost without Nella and realized I was still not comfortable talking about Mother. I quickly agreed, adding that Mother's passing had left a huge void in his life. It was all awkward and definitely a sign the evening needed to end. We said our good-byes.

Libby and I skipped arm in arm down Broadway. The lights reflected in Libby's big, beautiful blue eyes. We have had the time of our lives.

"Libby, how did we get so lucky to find each other? You do believe in destiny, right?"

"You do ask the most obvious and, I might add, the dumbest questions ever. Haven't you heard? Timing, my dear, is everything." Libby waited for my cue.

I responded without further prompt. "Speaking of time—Okay, kids, what time is it?"

"It's Howdy Doody time!" We simultaneously screamed at each other.

"Libby, you spit when you laugh just like you did when you were a kid."

"At least I don't spit when I eat and talk."

I was not done yet. "Okay. We are not allowed to eat, laugh or talk, at least not with other people."

We could not get our breath from laughing. Our stomachs ached, and our jaws ached, but our hearts soared. The streets were full of people now staring and giving us plenty of space on the sidewalk. Were we crazy or drunk or both? Either way, they wanted to give us a wide berth. Wow. That says a lot since you see everything on the streets of New York. Still, we were having too much fun to be intimidated. Our hearts were as light as we could ever wish for. This *was* Claire's and Libby's night.

When we entered our hotel, we gained momentum. "Hey, Miss Claire. We have that bottle of champagne still cold. What say we pop it and have some bubbly for a nightcap?"

"You have the best ideas." I could use a good, cold fizzy drink about now.

"Let's make a toast to the light of fresh beginnings and farewell to the darkness of the troubled past." Libby raised her crystal flute full of sparkling bubbly.

"Here, here. From your lips to my ears. I so raise my chalice in complete harmony."

Libby burst out laughing. "A simple clink of the glasses would do. You're starting to sound pompous—just like a lawyer."

"Well, you know what they say. If you can't convince 'em—"

"Yeah, yeah, I know—confuse 'em. Well, you did your job, counselor. Now, as boring as it sounds, we should write our article for the paper while Joanna is fresh on our minds."

"Wasn't she terrific?" It would be a shame to miss this opportunity to do our best work—some alcohol but not too much. I remembered our commitment.

"Libby, you know Mr. Kipperson at the Gazette is depending on us to fill space in the About Town section. Readers are bored with the same old local yokel gossip—who was at the latest family reunion and whose children were in town from college. *Stimulating stuff.* He was excited that we agreed to do this article on Joanna."

Libby's eyes looked glazed over, but she nodded in agreement.

"Libby, don't be shocked by this question, okay? But I was wondering about something. Remember how often Joanna and Dad were together after Johnny Mack died?"

"Yeah, so…"

"Do you think there was ever anything between them? I mean, she was young, but she was so worldly, and all, and my dad was impressed with her. She took the town by storm. Him included."

Libby could spot a trap and this definitely qualified. Had Claire heard rumors? She would protect her friend. Her face went blank as if by command. Years of practice hiding your emotions does have its benefits.

"Claire, let's put it this way. I don't deny that Joanna depended on your dad and there was something between them because they shared a bond. We all know that they were close, and he and Joanna are so much alike. But John Chastain isn't stupid. He wouldn't risk his family and everything he's built in that town for that." Libby had no intention of ending this day on a permanent sour note. She knew John Chastain, and he cared about Joanna like a daughter and was trying to help her. It seems that people have to have someone to talk about to add some zing to their own boring lives and to keep the gossip grapevine alive. The gossip wasn't true and she wouldn't be a party to it.

"That's what I thought but it has bothered me. I wondered what you thought. But deep down I know he was just trying to help Joanna through a tough time. Anyway, let's get busy and get that article done." She could depend on Libby for her no-nonsense, straight talk with no hidden meaning.

Local Star Lights up Broadway

Her name in lights! Anyone who knows her is not surprised. No need for a spotlight, Joanna Reyes continues to bedazzle and delight audiences each night in the long-running production of *Standing Room Only*. Her dancing delights whether tap dance, contemporary ballet, or chorus line high kicks. She does it all with equal ease and grace, solo or ensemble. Her strong, clear voice is made for the theater and with perfect pitch so that each theatergoer hears every word. She will knock you out of your seat with the high notes and captivate you with her low, sultry whisper soft notes. Her brilliant stage presence outshines the spotlight illuminating the entire theater, even to the back row.

Joanna was born in southern California and spent most of her childhood in Los Angeles. She is the daughter of famed movie producer Reynaldo Reyes. She was an ensemble performer in high school at the Hollywood Playhouse and acted in various productions at the Center Stage and Casa Del Sol theaters. She has starred in two off-Broadway musical comedy productions prior to her singing and dancing role in *Standing Room Only* and received rave reviews.

Joanna Reyes lived in our town for two years with her aunt Delores Delgado and attended the local high school. She had the starring role in both her Junior and Senior plays and competed in the one-act play State competition, placing third. She was involved in many civic activities and volunteered at the hospital. She encouraged her peers through her example to be involved with their community. She is loved and respected by her many friends here who are thrilled for her and her success in New York. We are proud of our Broadway star. Shine, Joanna, shine!

Claire Chastain and Libby Callaghan

We looked at each other and shook our heads. It was past time for sleep. We had overindulged with too much champagne and too much excitement. We both accepted what time it was. It was time to go home, and a time for new beginnings. Libby would teach ninth grade English at her old school but in a brand new building. She and Angela were working on making Camp Callaghan Kids a reality. They were getting the word out. Several other local ranchers liked the idea: they were starting their own kid camps for disadvantaged kids.

"Good night Libby. I love you more than you can ever know."

"Good night Miss Claire. I do know because I love you more."

The next morning, Libby and I had finished packing and were ready to walk out the door when the phone rang in our hotel room. It was Michael.

"Good Morning, Sunshine. I'm glad I caught you before you left. Is your plane still as scheduled?"

"Yes, as far as I know. We are packed and ready. Oh, Michael, we had a wonderful trip. I can't wait to get home and tell you. Joanna and New York were unbelievable."

"I'm so glad you two enjoyed yourselves. You were way overdue for some fun. I'll pick you guys up at the airport so don't get lost in New York. I'm ready for you to come home. I miss you."

"Michael, you don't sound right. Is there something wrong?"

"No, just hurry home. Need my honey back." Claire was not convinced. She had known Michael long enough to hear trouble in his voice. *A storm after the calm.*

Chapter 30. Lifeblood & Legacy

After all these years, I should know better. But yet, I still allowed myself to fall into a momentary lapse and then I'm surprised and shocked that life happens without warning. I wanted to give up everything and do nothing. Totally unprepared and vulnerable, I felt displaced, aimless and hopeless. All that had made me who I am had been stripped away. I felt exposed and bare to the bone, raw and open. I had just buried my father. Now the cold, imposing marble of the double headstone awaited: it was ready for the stonecutter. John and Nella reunited. During her long illness, we realized that Mother's days would be few. Dad was taken suddenly and without warning. He suffered a massive heart attack and was likely gone when he hit the floor. Either way, I was not prepared to function in a world without my family. I adored them. For the first time, I had an inkling of how Libby must have felt when she lost her family.

Through my tears of sorrow and loss, I had much to be grateful for this day. I remembered my mother's soft admonition—always be grateful for your blessings. The relationship with my dad had suffered a tremendous blow and an estrangement that threatened to destroy us. I thanked God for bringing us together before he was taken away. I took comfort that he and I had made the commitment to rebuild our trust in each other and to make us strong again. God did not see fit for us to have the opportunity to make that happen. In this whole process with Dad and Lorene, I had recognized my own weaknesses as well as those of my father. By setting my father on a pedestal, I had set him up for failure and myself up for disappointment. In spite of his shortcomings, he would always be my hero. I was proud of him. But I was angry at him for leaving me and for leaving me alone to deal with Lorene. My mother's sweet voice whispered to me even now. The burden I carried could be lightened. I had to be free and let go of my resentment. I must forgive Lorene and my dad for every wrong I stubbornly believed I had a right to hang onto. Remind you of anyone, Claire? I was unquestionably my father's daughter.

I thanked God for the love my parents and I shared. I was a blessed child who had lived a life full of love and hope. I lived a blessed life. I felt that I was equipped to cope with Lorene and everything she would throw my way. I also felt prepared for life's challenges. It would not be easy, but I would manage. I thought back to the people in my life who were worthy of my respect and admiration—parents, teachers, and friends. My loving parents tirelessly tried to instill values that could withstand the test of time and hardship—a code that I could live by. My teachers took an interest in all their students and valued their profession as a calling. Their greatest gift was their compassion and teaching us to think. All these people gave me the tools I needed to grow up and be independent. *I knew what I was made of.* I was responsible for myself. There was no one else to look to, to lay blame on, to make demands of or to depend upon. I was self-sufficient and provided for myself. I could build a life to be proud of and leave a legacy of my own. I experienced the unfamiliar feeling of having strength that I was unaware of. I acknowledged that I was bound to a Higher Power.

As I drove through my town, I was content. I saw the changes, but I was cradled in my memories. My town looked hauntingly similar to my first memory of it. Perhaps the changes blurred because I was so familiar with it. A gleaming glass and brick modern one-story high school had taken the place of our old dark and dreary red brick building which had towered some three stories over the playground, outdoor basketball court and track. I saw that we had made progress in important ways. I remember all those days that our classmate Nina struggled to climb the stairs with her heavy leg brace weighing her body down making it almost impossible for her to maneuver the stairs. A car accident had left her severely injured but alive. After months of rehabilitation, she was left with disfigurement, a massive brace, and an arduous gait as forever reminders of her childhood ordeal. We helped her by carrying her books and supplies and making trips up and down the stairs for her, but she had to make the strenuous trip up and down the stairs several times a day. Now we had a superb new school for our most precious resources. I smiled. Lucky little stinkers, too, since Libby was the new ninth-grade teacher in the new school.

Many of the buildings in town were the same as for the last hundred years but, instead of looking old and tired, they appeared renewed. Storefronts had been freshly painted and sported new signs. There were few vacant buildings which reassured that people were drawn to this town. My father loved this place to distraction. He had devoted much of his life to making it a respectable and pleasant place to live. He was a leader who spent countless hours and energy in every civic organization. I was drowning in the images. Everywhere I looked was a reminder of him and his loving, hard-working hand. He led the way for us and pushed for needed change whether popular or vigorously resisted. His tireless work on the hospital board for over twenty years had come to fruition. The new hospital gleamed as state-of-the-art with the latest technology, equipment and staff. He had been honored with the other members of the board whose pictures lined the hallway. These men and women were the founders whose efforts and fundraising were in large part responsible for the new hospital—symbols of hard work and never-ending allegiance. They refused to allow this place to end up a pathetic ghost of a town like so many others. The leaders continually pumped life and vitality into their community seeking out new business opportunities along with the citizens who worked and contributed to our town—the connective tissue that unites, shapes and strengthens a community.

Whether we choose lives of anonymity or strive to arrive at the top of the local "A list" (or somewhere in between), our lives are destined to intersect. My memories burst before me like a brilliant slideshow flashing snapshots—people and events of a life unfolding poignant and meaningful. The events and personal encounters of our lives may seem disjointed and haphazard, but ultimately we can see the intricacies if we have a desire to do so. The seemingly mismatched pieces of our individual giant puzzles do fit. Looking back, I see how my reactions to life's events helped to form my values and beliefs. How easy it is to lose sight of *the meaningful* and how difficult it can be to make a *life*. Is that what life amounts to—our personal series of mundane distractions in a wasteland of material possessions and obsessions?

The old boarding house stood erect and still stylish with its wraparound porch proudly showing rows of wispy ferns hanging from their baskets as if time stood still. I was relieved to see that it had not been torn down, but instead had been renewed and kept presentable. It was the 1960s all over again. The brightly painted Adirondack chairs even now patiently waited in position for the old men and women to come sit for a spell under the giant oaks. I can hear my dad's deep velvet voice to me as a youngster, "Claire, you know, so and so's (the great movie star) dad has lived in that boarding house for years. She still comes from Hollywood to visit him." He winked and grinned. I remembered one day when I saw a long black limo stretched along the entire length of the gravel driveway of the gingerbread house. I envisioned the glamorous creature within and thought how glorious if she would give me her autograph, although I never got up enough nerve to stop and ask. I decided it was best not to bother her. After all, my getting her autograph was not that important. I smiled. Libby would have asked for her autograph and have gotten it. "After all, Claire, she's on our territory." I imagined her reply.

My dear Libby and how she has changed my life. Her survival, strength and hope inspired and became part of me. It was our backgrounds as adopted children that drove me to find a rewarding career in family law.

Out the state highway, a new sign reflected in the bright sunlight, Pop. 2138. The latest census reflected a hearty increase in residents thanks to revitalization. The government had built a new power plant and numerous oil and gas wells had been discovered. Real estate was a booming business. Land was worth fifty times what it sold for fifteen years ago. A nine-hole public golf course had been built on the rolling hills outside town with its own small restaurant and pro shop. Now that I was hooked on hitting and then finding the perplexing white ball, I was excited to see it. There was so much to love about this place.

I slowly continued outside town to my favorite haunt out to the lake.

The car window was down, wind blowing my hair and the radio playing, the sun glistening on the water. Not much had changed in some ways. I was sixteen again. The winding, narrow road was marked by familiar *parking* spots worn bare by years of young lovers who had parked to admire the scenery and whatever came next. I pulled in and parked by the pavilion. In my mind, I heard the music of Chuck Berry blasting away. Rick Nelson was cranking out *Garden Party* and was in good tune today. Most of our high school dances were held here at the old pavilion overlooking the small but serene and protected lake. What a comfort that, all these years later, there was still the quiet of no motor boats.

I gave in to flooding emotion and cried like a baby who wouldn't stop. I was overcome by every moment of joy and relief; every hateful thought; every moment of terror and heartache; every moment of sadness, disbelief and frustration; every moment of hope and shame that I had felt for all those years that I had lived in this place. I cried for all the connected lives and those that were not connected and should have been. It was my turn to fulfill my own commitment and legacy. I must keep my promise. I listened to my soul speak and was comforted. My time here was not done. The realization hit me full force. I accepted reality; this is the place of my roots. No, it will never be the same without my dear mother and father. I acknowledged and accepted it instead of fighting against it.

There was a calm reassurance that I had come full circle. I was granted permission to let go of the unmet expectations, the guilt and bad feelings of the past—all *shattered illusions*. The weighty cloak of *darkness* gave way. In its place, a refreshing lightness took hold. My spirit at once sparked alive and enlightened. I was grateful for the time and place in which I was born and grew up whether by mere chance or destiny. I could not pretend I was untouched by this place—it was a cherished place deep in my heart. Life without my father would be strange, sad and empty, but still could be worthwhile and meaningful. I will always be a *blessed* daughter of this town.

Our own hideous reminder of man's inhumanity to man—the pus pocket of the town—had long ago been bulldozed away and its residents sent packing to blend into civilization. Integration had, at last, come to our town and taken away the tiny despicable shacks and deplorable way of life imposed upon the black residents of our town. Their children were no longer forced to be bused away to school and away from white town. People were now compelled to do what they should have done naturally and humanely hundreds of years ago. This was a sign of progress however slow and painful but still a shameful reminder—we did not act like human beings and do the right thing without the government forcing us to do so. Here was a town that took pride in taking care of its own and yet never reached out to do the right thing by all our residents, especially the children.

Whether by commission or omission, I was a citizen of that town and ashamed of my own complacency. We could not undo the wrong, but we must not repeat it. What was once an ugly block of human offense, decay and deterioration, shined before me as a glistening, thoughtful place. A picturesque park with benches and fountains and green space was offered as a reminder and a place of quiet solitude. A newcomer would not know the town's history except for the large black and white photographs of the old shantytown encased in glass beside a marble and brass plaque of dedication.

Throughout my life, the power and pervasive spirit of hope has been a constant force of nature. No matter how helpless or beaten I may feel, there arises in me a revival of hope. It continually returns and sustains me, and I cling to it—hope that refuses to be destroyed. We see it every day. We are surrounded by people who keep hope alive no matter how grievous the tragedy or hopeless the circumstances. No matter how desolate or wretched we become, no matter how many mistakes and offenses against each other we commit, no matter the dark hopelessness with which the evildoers relentlessly scheme to cloak our world, there continues an enduring outcry for *hope* and *faith* in the Almighty as we continue our journey.

Miriam C. Crouch lives in Irving, Texas with her husband, Gilbert, a retired Irving firefighter. She grew up in Texas and graduated from Texas Christian University. *Daughter of the Town* is a celebration of family, friendship, Texas and the small town way of life in an inspiring story of hope and forgiveness.

Thank you so much for reading one of our **Literary Fiction** novels.
If you enjoyed our book, please check out our recommended title for your
next great read!

The Five Wishes by Mr. Murray McBride by Joe Siple

2018 Maxy Award "Book of the Year"

"A sweet...tale of human connection...will feel familiar to fans of Hallmark

movies." *–KIRKUS REVIEWS*

"An emotional story that will leave readers meditating on the life-saving
magic of kindness." *–Indie Reader*

View other Black Rose Writing titles at www.blackrosewriting.com/books

and use promo code **PRINT** to receive a **20% discount** when purchasing.